The Thin Blue Line Series

FIVE ROSES FOR WALTER

LeeAnne James

Black Rose Writing | Texas

ISBN: 978-1-68513-677-2
LIBRARY OF CONGRESS CONTROL NUMBER: 2025939116
PUBLISHED BY BLACK ROSE WRITING
www.blackrosewriting.com

Printed in the United States of America
Suggested Retail Price (SRP) $21.95

Five Roses for Walter is printed in Calluna

*As a planet-friendly publisher, Black Rose Writing does its best to eliminate unnecessary waste to reduce paper usage and energy costs, while never compromising the reading experience. As a result, the final word count vs. page count may not meet common expectations.

DEDICATION

This was a difficult novel to write. After spending over thirty years working with law enforcement officers, I've learned just how much depravity there is in the world, but sexual abusers are among the worst.

I dedicate this book to those who were victimized by these abusers and to those who arrest and prosecute them.

If you are a victim of sexual abuse or know of an abuse that's happening, call the National Sexual Abuse Hotline, operated by the Rape, Abuse & Incest National Network (RAINN) at 1-800-656-HOPE (1-800-656-4673). The call is confidential and free.

ACKNOWLEDGEMENTS

I'd like to thank my husband, Bill, and my son, BJ, for helping me as my various manuscripts came to life. I've always said, "everything can always be tweaked," and they've helped me tweak my books until the results were as good as they could be. It was truly a group effort.

I would also like to thank MEB for her talent and skill as an editor. You've put the polish on this story until it shone. I am indebted to you.

And of course, where would I be without the Black Rose Writing staff? A huge thank you goes out to Reagan and his team, as well as the other BRW authors. The support is phenomenal.

Thank you all.

Five Roses
For
Walter

"I can be changed by what happens to me. But I refuse to be reduced by it."
–Maya Angelou

"Tomorrow hopes we have learned something from yesterday."
–John Wayne

Prologue

October 6, 1961
The state of affairs was tense between the United States and the Soviet Union. President John F. Kennedy urged American citizens to build underground bomb shelters to protect them from atomic fallout if there were ever a nuclear exchange with the Soviets.

Exactly one year later, our government discovered that the Soviet Union had placed nuclear missiles in Cuba and the world watched closely as the Cuban Missile Crisis unfolded. Fearing the worst, those Americans who had listened to Kennedy the year before made sure they had enough canned goods and other non-perishable items stockpiled in their new backyard bomb shelters, just in case they would have to hunker down for an extended period of time.

Although the missile exchange with the Soviet Union never came to fruition, many of these concrete bunkers are still around today.

CHAPTER ONE

Eight-year-old Stevie Deerhunter was excited about the upcoming Halloween party at school, and he'd just asked his older sister, Joanie, to help him with his costume for what seemed to Joanie like the thousandth time.

"I told you I would help you and I will, but right now, I've got homework to do," she scolded him. "Stop bugging me about it and leave me alone for a while! I need to get this done."

She regretted her words as soon as they left her mouth when she saw the hurt in her little brother's eyes. A tiny hiccup escaped his lips as his chin quivered. Before she could apologize, he ran from the room. She stood up from the kitchen table intending to follow him, but the slam of his bedroom door told her she wouldn't be allowed in.

Stevie rarely closed his door, and almost never slammed it. He didn't like being alone—in fact, he avoided solitude at all costs. So, for him to shut his bedroom door in that way, Joanie knew in her heart she had hurt her little brother deeply.

Joanie gathered up her ninth-grade math book, notebook, and pencil from the kitchen table with an audible sigh and stuffed them into her backpack. Homework would have to wait. She was feeling guilty about blowing up at Stevie, so she wouldn't be able to concentrate on her homework, anyway. The words she had spoken replayed in her mind in an endless loop.

She checked the pocket in her worn jeans and found the $10 bill her mother had given her that morning towards Stevie's costume. Glancing at the grease-speckled clock on the wall over the stove, she decided that if she hurried, she could get the necessary costume supplies from the dollar store and be back home in time to help with dinner. That would give her plenty of time after dinner to put the costume together with Stevie and still get her homework done. It might be a late night, but she'd worry about that later.

She headed outside, so excited to be making amends for snapping at Stevie that she forgot to put on her jacket. On her walk to the store, the fall air was chilly, but fourteen-year-old Joanie welcomed the bite she felt on her bare arms. Her long, black hair was twisted into a messy bun on top of her head, allowing the breeze to wrap its icy fingers around her neck. She deserved to be cold, she thought. It served her right for being so mean. *I hate it when I get upset with Stevie,* she thought. *I never should have yelled at him.*

In her mind, Joanie again replayed the hurtful words she had spoken to her younger brother.

Joanie fought to keep the tears from spilling from her eyes, but eventually they won, leaving a wet path down her cheeks before landing on her T-shirt. She swiped at the tears with her palms, walking with her head down and putting her hands in her front jeans pockets, deep in thought. If she had looked up, she would have seen the car trailing slowly behind her. When she entered the store, the car parked at the curb.

It took only a few minutes searching the aisles of the dollar store before Joanie found the makeup she would need to turn her little brother into a zombie for Halloween. She picked out white paint for his face, a thick black pencil to form shadows around his eyes, and a tube of fake blood she would apply to look as if it was dripping from his mouth. She even found a set of plastic teeth that were supposed to resemble vampire teeth, but she knew he would wear them, anyway. As she selected her purchases, a smile slowly formed on her lips.

He would put on some old jeans and a shirt that no longer fit him, and to make the clothes more zombie-like, Joanie would rip holes in them until they looked raggedy. She smiled even more as she envisioned Stevie as a stiff-legged zombie with his arms outstretched in front of him, as he approached their neighbors' doors, looking for candy to fill his plastic pumpkin.

After paying for her items, Joanie left the store and turned towards home. Happier, now that she'd be making amends with Stevie, she had a skip in her step as she began the walk home.

This time she noticed the slow-moving car that seemed to be following her. She glanced at the car out of the corner of her eye, trying to be subtle. She knew little about cars, but this one seemed to be kind of old. The driver, an older man wearing large wire-rimmed glasses, waved at her.

Joanie focused her eyes on the sidewalk in front of her and quickened her step. The man pulled his car closer to the curb next to her and hollered something through the open passenger-side window that she didn't understand. She stopped and looked at him.

"What?" she asked loudly.

He got out of the car, and with a friendly smile, approached Joanie on the sidewalk.

"You looked pretty upset a few minutes ago. Are you okay?" he asked.

"Yeah, I'm fine." She was surprised the man would have noticed when she herself had already forgotten about the tears.

"Can I give you a lift home?" the man asked. "You look like you're in a hurry."

"No, that's okay. Thank you, anyway." Her mother would be pleased that Joanie was being so polite.

"Listen," the man said, "I'm headed in that direction anyway, so as long as I'm going that way, I'll give you a lift." He reached out and gently wrapped his hand around her elbow. "I promise I won't bite."

Joanie looked at the gentleman, who looked to be about her father's age. He was wearing a light jacket, zipped halfway, but it looked like he was wearing a nice polo shirt underneath. While most of the men in her family wore blue jeans, even at work, this man was wearing khaki pants, as if he was a salesman or a doctor or someone important. His wide smile revealed straight, white teeth.

After assessing the man, Joanie said, "Well, I guess that would be okay. I am in kind of a hurry."

"Great. Let me help you with your things while you get in the car, okay?" The man took the package from her hand, opened the passenger side door, and let her slide into the front seat. He tossed the bag of makeup into the back, not apparently caring that the contents spilled onto the seat. He sat behind the wheel of the car and glanced at her, still flashing a smile. "Don't forget to buckle up. I don't want you getting hurt."

"Okay." She watched out the windshield as he pulled away from the curb.

Joanie gave the man her address and pointed in the general direction of her home, telling him he could turn right at the next block.

"So," he said, "what did you get at the store? Anything interesting?"

"Well, my little brother wants to be a zombie for Halloween, so I got him some makeup and a set of vampire teeth. I think he'll like that." She smiled at the thought.

"How old is your little brother?"

"He's only eight. He can be a pain sometimes, but I don't mind. I kind of take care of him a lot because my parents work most of the time."

Only then did she realize the man had driven past her street. "Hey, wait," she said, pointing out the side window. "You just passed my street."

"I was going to take you for a treat first. I thought you might like some ice cream."

"No, I don't want any ice cream. I want to go home." Her head swiveled between the man and the view out the side window, and she began to panic. "Mister, please. I need to get home. They're waiting for me. I have to help my mother fix dinner, then I need to help Stevie with his costume, and then I have to finish my homework."

The man kept driving, ignoring Joanie's pleading. She began to cry. "Please, mister. I want to go home."

"I'm taking you to a new home. You'll like it." He gave Joanie a sideways glance. His wide smile from before had turned into a tight-lipped grimace. She was scared and cried harder.

"Please, mister, take me home."

Pleading steadily, Joanie received no further comments from the man. He continued to drive with his eyes glued to the front windshield, without answering her questions or looking in her direction.

Staring at his profile, a strange look was plastered on his face, like a creepy clown in a horror film.

Her mind was racing, looking for an escape from this nightmare. Instinctively, her hand found the door handle and pulled to no avail. The latch mechanism was broken, making the handle useless. She was trapped. Goosebumps broke out on her arms; a chill ran down her spine. Her fear threatened to consume her like a cold, suffocating blanket.

Joanie spotted a man on the sidewalk as they drove past. She banged on the side window, her palms flat against the glass, hoping to get his attention. The man was too engrossed in the cell phone cradled in his hand to notice the desperate pleas of the young girl in the car.

They drove for about fifteen minutes, although it felt to Joanie like so much longer. Finally, the man turned into a driveway that cut through a tall hedge row of arborvitae. The thick green bushes separated the front yard from the roadway and kept the house almost entirely hidden from the view of passing motorists. Joanie focused on the single-story ranch home that suddenly appeared in front of her.

Joanie turned to the man and quietly said, "Please, mister, let me go. I won't tell anyone, I promise."

The man turned off the car and walked around to the passenger side door. "Take off the seatbelt, please."

Shaking almost uncontrollably, she struggled to unlatch the seat belt until her jittery fingers finally found the release. Reluctantly, she got out of the car, still pleading for her freedom. He grabbed her roughly by the arm and led the way to the front door of the home. She tried to pull back, but it was no use. He maintained a firm grip on her arm and had a longer stride, causing her to frog march to the front door.

"I don't want any ice cream, and I don't want to go to your house! I want to go home. Please!" Joanie screamed.

"Shut up. We don't want the neighbors to hear you, now do we?" the man said through clenched teeth.

He turned the knob, and the unlocked door swung open easily. Joanie looked around at what appeared to be a living room. Tall piles of newspapers and dozens of beer bottles and cans were scattered around the room, with some detritus covering the end tables, while most of it littered the floor. There were piles and piles of every type and size of paper imaginable. Envelopes, letters, and even skinny papers that looked like grocery-store receipts covered every available space throughout the room. The junk on the floor was arranged in a way that allowed just enough space to walk through the mess.

Joanie struggled to pull away from him, but the fourteen-year-old girl was no match for the grown man. He held onto her arm, digging his fingers tightly into her flesh. Her ardent pleas had turned into soft whimpers.

The man led her down a carpeted hallway, through a door that opened into the garage, and down a set of wooden stairs into the basement. Four small windows, situated high on opposing walls, allowed only a minimal amount of light into the dark and dank room, but it was enough that they could see the way.

Joanie looked around the basement in amazement as they wound their way past dozens of wooden shelving units that held hundreds, if not thousands, of beer cans and bottles. It wasn't possible to tell from the cans, but some bottles appeared full, others were empty. The shelves were set up in tight, nonsensical clusters, forcing them to walk in a mixed-up zig-zag pattern to get to the opposite end of the basement.

The man stopped in front of an empty metal rack that looked very much out of place compared to the rest of the cluttered wooden shelves. Taking one step behind her, he switched from holding her with his right hand to the left. She took the second of opportunity and bolted through the basement towards the garage.

She ran, weaving between the racks, not sure which way was out. She could hear him close behind, his shoes making slapping sounds on the cement floor. Suddenly, she felt before she saw his arms grab her around her waist. He lifted her off the ground and carried her back to the bare metal rack, her back wedged tight to his chest. She tried kicking, but all she connected with was a few bottles and cans.

Once they reached the same empty rack as before, he set her down. "I would advise you not to try that again. I'm being patient with you, but I can get very angry, very fast, and you don't want to find out what happens when I get angry."

Then, with his left hand wrapped tightly around Joanie's arm, he used his right to pull the rack away from the wall, exposing a door. He pulled a set of keys from his pants pocket and unlocked the deadbolt attached to the door. Holding the door open with his hip, he reached into the opening to flip a light switch on the wall. A single, bare bulb on a short cord dangled from the ceiling, casting a yellow shadow, the only light.

Joanie could see a small, barren room, about the size of a small closet, with another door facing them on the opposite wall. Wordlessly, the man pushed Joanie forward. The door slammed shut behind them, and Joanie jumped.

This time, the man used the fingers of his free hand to spin the dial on a combination padlock on the second door. The lock popped open, and with a loud creaking noise, he pulled the door open to expose another closet-sized area, even smaller than the first. The opposite wall had a dark rectangular hole carved into it.

To Joanie, the opening looked like a large mouse hole, about as tall as her little brother. She couldn't see what lay beyond the opening.

As they stood in front of the hole, the man took the padlock and moved it from the outside of the door to the inside and spun the dial to relock the padlock. They were now locked in. The room was barely big enough for the two of them.

"Get in there," said the man, as he pointed towards the hole and pushed her forward.

"Please, mister. Don't make me get in there. Please let me go home." Joanie was white with fear. Her voice dropped to a whisper. "Please! I promise I won't tell."

"Get in there," he said, louder this time.

"What's in there? I can't see. It's too dark, and I don't want to go in there," she pleaded.

The man didn't answer. He just pointed to the opening and gave her a firm push on her back. With no other options available to her, Joanie took one step forward. She hesitated and looked back at the man. His eyes were wide, and he licked his lips.

She turned away from him and took a small step towards the hole in the wall. All she could see was what looked to be a tunnel beyond the opening.

Cautiously looking into the darkness, she could see only a few feet inside the tunnel. From what she could see of the first few feet, all four sides appeared to be made from cement blocks. When she moved closer and stood directly in front of the hole, the shaft became even darker, with her body blocking the light from behind.

She felt his hand on her back as he prodded her to move forward. She leaned forward and bent her neck to avoid smacking her head on the low ceiling of the tunnel.

"No, not like that. You have to crawl in backwards. Get on the floor, on your hands and knees."

Joanie's stomach was tight, and she fought the urge to vomit. She'd never been so frightened in her entire life. She hesitated but did as she was told and got on the ground. Her tears fell from her cheeks, leaving dark, round splotches on the cement floor.

Joanie slowly crawled feet first into the shaft, her sobs echoing off the close walls. She couldn't see what was around her as she carefully crept backward. She used her hands and feet to feel her way along the cold, hard concrete.

She was afraid of spiders and her one thought was to hope there weren't any spiders in the darkened tunnel.

After a few moments, she realized she'd come to the end of the tunnel when she could no longer feel the floor behind her. She used the tips of her feet to confirm nothing solid was beneath them. Her foot dangled in mid-air as if she'd reached the edge of a cliff.

"There's a stepladder you can use to climb down," the man said. She jumped when he spoke so close to her. Because of the pitch-black darkness, she hadn't realized he had crawled in after her.

Inching backwards, Joanie slowly lowered her foot over the edge to find the first step. She carefully backed down the ladder, and after three steps, she placed her feet firmly on the floor. It was very dark. She had no idea where she was, so she simply stood still, too afraid to move.

"Stay right there," came the man's voice beside her. She felt his hands grab onto her shoulders and shift her to the side. A familiar sound nearby reminded her of the quick flick of a lighter, similar to the lighter her father used to ignite the kindling in their wood stove. Suddenly, a small flame flicked at her side. It illuminated the man's face in a ghostly shadow. He walked a few feet away from her and used the flame to light a small camping lantern.

"This is your new home," the man said, smiling. Horrified, she looked around. She stood in a room about twelve feet square, with eight-foot ceilings. The floor, ceiling, and windowless walls were made of concrete. To her left was an old-fashioned, claw-foot bathtub on a low wooden platform that sat about eighteen inches off the ground.

She wrinkled her nose at the damp, musty smell. It reminded her of her grandfather's stone-walled basement after it had been raining for a few days.

Towards the back of the room was an open doorway. She couldn't make out the details of what lay beyond the unlit opening, but perhaps, she thought, it led to the outdoors. Her feet seemed to move on their own as she walked towards the doorway.

She was sad to see the doorway led into another enclosed room, about the same size as the first room. The man followed with the lantern and set it in the doorway between the two rooms.

Both rooms added together seemed to be about the size of her living room back home. No windows or doors would lead to her freedom in this room, either.

Glancing around the second room, tears began to sting her eyes. Against the back wall was a foam mattress lying on the floor. No bed frame, no sheets, no blankets, just a thin, dirty mattress.

Joanie turned and ran towards the stepladder and the only way out of the nightmare she'd gotten herself into. He grabbed her around the waist and easily stopped her. "Oh, no you don't. You're here to stay, and we're going to be good friends from now on."

As the man lifted her off the ground, Joanie kicked and thrashed, trying to break free of his hold, but he was too strong. He carried her back to the other room and pushed her down onto the mattress. Before she could get up, he sat on top of her, straddling her legs and pinning her to the mattress. She could feel the cold of the floor through the thin foam. Terrified, she screamed as loud as she could.

He pushed his mouth onto hers and forced his tongue into her mouth, silencing her screams. She almost gagged. He was kissing her hard enough that her teeth cut into her lips. As he lifted his head, breaking the kiss, she gulped for air. He looked down at her and smiled.

He held one of her wrists over her head. Joanie heard the clank of metal as a handcuff was clamped onto her wrist. Then he did the same thing with the other wrist. She bent her head back to look at her hands and saw that the handcuffs were anchored to the wall with a chain. With her hands subdued, she was at his mercy.

She tried bucking him off, but he was sitting firmly on her legs. With his weight on her knees, she couldn't move. She felt him fumbling with the button of her jeans and then found the zipper. He slid his hand under her panties and his fingers found her most private area. She screamed louder, begging him to stop.

With the other hand, he lifted the front of her shirt above her breasts. His hand went to her breast and squeezed. She clenched her teeth in pain. She tried thrashing back and forth, but his weight on top of her was enough to hold her down. His hand went inside her jeans again, and he worked her jeans and underwear down her legs.

He reached for his own pants and unzipped them. With his knees, he separated her thighs and entered her. At fourteen years old, she had never had any sexual experiences of any kind and was a virgin. She gulped as he tore into her, the pain beyond anything she'd ever experienced. Stars swirled in front of her eyes just before her world went dark. She passed out as he continued to thrust into her.

CHAPTER TWO

When Joanie woke up, she was unsure of where she was. She blinked, trying to get her bearings. All she knew was she was so very cold. She looked down at her body and realized she was naked. Suddenly, the pieces of the nightmare came flooding back in her mind—shopping for Stevie's Halloween makeup, getting into a man's car, being driven to the man's home, crawling through a tunnel into a concrete room, and the unimaginable—being raped at the hands of a total stranger.

As she looked around, she could see from the dimly lit lamp that she was, thankfully, alone. She spotted a pile of clothes that she recognized as her clothes, lying on the floor across the room. She stretched out her legs to try and grab them, but because she was still chained to the wall, she wasn't able to reach them.

Joanie sat up and edged her back into the corner of the room as closely as the handcuffs and chains would allow. She raised her knees to her chest and wrapped her arms around her legs.

Her body hurt in places where it shouldn't. Joanie was ashamed, humiliated, and disgusted. *How could this be happening?* She needed to get home to her parents and Stevie. Her family was counting on her to help around the house. She rested her forehead on her knees and cried.

Joanie thought she heard a noise. She stopped crying and lifted her head. Yes, definitely a noise. She was barely breathing, trying to remain still so she could listen.

"Hello. How are you, my precious Little Flower?" The man who'd kidnapped her, raped her, and stolen her innocence, stood smiling in the doorway.

Fearfully, she pulled her knees into her chest even tighter. She hoped her legs covered her privates and breasts.

"I brought you some dinner. I thought you might be hungry." The man had a Tupperware container in one hand, a plastic cup in the other. He set the cup on a plastic milk crate next to her. He took the lid off the container and tipped it to show her the food that was in it. "Do you like baked chicken?"

She didn't answer him.

He pulled a packet of utensils from his back pocket—the kind wrapped in a plastic sleeve that comes with fast-food meals. "Oh, there's no need to be upset with me. We're going to be great friends. By the way, my name is Walter. You can call me Walt."

She didn't care what his name was. "Let me go. I want to go home," she said angrily. The intense hate she felt for this man was a strong feeling she'd never known before. It consumed her. It consumed her. She could feel the hatred in every cell in her body.

"No, you're not going home. You're staying with me now, and I'm going to take good care of you." He tried to smooth her hair, the way a parent might console an upset child, but she pulled her head away from him.

He looked at her for a moment. Finally, he asked, "Do you love your brother? His name is Stevie, right?"

With the mention of Stevie's name, Joanie's eyes opened wide.

"Remember, you had given me your address, so I know where your family lives. You need to be a good girl for me, or else Stevie might get hurt."

The room spun as Joanie comprehended the threat to her only sibling. "Don't hurt Stevie. Please, don't hurt my little brother," she pleaded.

"As long as you behave like a good girl and do what you're told, he won't get hurt." As he spoke, Joanie watched in horror as Walt reached for the zipper on his pants.

After Walt had raped her for the second time that day, he removed the handcuffs and let her put her clothes back on. He led her into the first room and turned on a tall floor lamp that was standing in the corner. The lamp held a single bulb but no shade.

"I thought you might like a lamp instead of that old camping lantern. Wasn't that a nice idea?" She refused to answer him.

He showed her the toilet that she was to use. To her, it looked like the kind that old people used, with a toilet seat attached to an aluminum frame, except, instead of a bowl underneath, this one had a large paint bucket to catch the waste. The idea of using it horrified her.

"I brought you a clock radio you can listen to," he said. "It might not pick up a lot of stations, but you can try.

"I hope you have a good night, my Little Flower." As he left, he picked up the camping lantern, extinguished the flame, and took it with him. He turned back to her and said, "Don't forget to eat your dinner."

Joanie watched her captor disappear into the tunnel. She heard the door slam at the other end. "Let me out! Please!" she screamed. Tears streamed down her face.

Joanie ran towards the tunnel and waited, even though she knew deep down he wouldn't be coming back. After a few moments, she climbed the stepladder, quietly placing one foot at a time on each step. She listened, but the only thing she heard was her own heartbeat. She closed her eyes, silently praying he wouldn't return and catch her.

In the darkness of the tunnel, Joanie crept forward, inching her way bit by bit. Her hands led the way as she patted the cold concrete floor. She finally reached the door and sat up on her knees. The door felt rough to her hands as she searched for the doorknob. The back of her hand connected with the knob in a loud, metallic thump. Joanie held her breath.

After a few moments, Walt hadn't returned, so she tried the doorknob. It turned, but the door did not open. It was then she remembered the padlock. She raised her hand and found the hasp where the lock had been. He must have moved it to the other side. She sat back on her haunches, her chin resting on her chest, and let the tears flow. She carefully crawled back through the tunnel.

Walt stood on the opposite side of the door and watched as the knob twisted back and forth. He smiled.

She was alone in the cold, damp room. She looked at her surroundings, still not able to believe the nightmare that was happening to her.

Joanie ignored the baked chicken. She wasn't hungry. More pressing was the need to go to the bathroom. She cringed at the thought of peeing into the contraption made of a toilet seat positioned over a bucket, but with no other options available, she was forced to use it. At least he'd left her a roll of toilet paper.

When Joanie was finished, she returned to the back room and lay on the mattress. She curled up in a ball and quietly cried. Within minutes, blessed sleep came over her.

Joanie woke up to someone shaking her shoulder. "Wake up, Little Flower. C'mon. It's time to wake up."

She sat up, rubbing her eyes. The tears from the night before had left her eyes scratchy and crusty.

"I see that you didn't eat your chicken. I don't appreciate that, Joanie." Walt looked at her, his lips pinched into a straight line. "Groceries cost a lot of money these days, and I don't like to waste anything. Anything! Do you understand me?"

"I'm sorry," she said quietly. After the trauma of being kidnapped and raped,

Joanie had been too upset to eat. However, based on the harshness of his tone, she didn't think she should admit that.

"Just don't let it happen again. When I bring you food, I expect you to eat it. Got that?" He spoke softer this time but still firmly.

"Yes, sir." Joanie was trying hard not to cry.

"Okay. Now, it's time to show you what I want you to do. We'll start with a bath. Doesn't that sound nice?"

Joanie didn't answer him. The idea of taking a bath in front of the man that raped her terrified her. She fought hard to keep the tears at bay, but they still fell from her eyes. "Please, mister…"

"Mister? Why are you calling me 'mister?' I told you, you can call me Walt." He held out his hand, as if to help her rise from the mattress. She ignored his gesture and got to her feet on her own. He reached out, grabbed her hand, and led her into the first room.

"There's a hose right here that you can use to fill the tub." Joanie's eyes followed his hand as he gestured to the green tube coming from the ceiling. He reached up and turned the spigot at the end of the hose. Water flowed into the tub and onto the floor.

"Oops! I forgot the plug. We don't want to waste any water, now do we?" He put a plastic plug into the drain and quietly stood watching the water flow from the garden hose into the old porcelain tub.

After a brief minute, he turned off the water. "Okay, get in the tub."

Joanie looked at him wide-eyed as he stood in front of her, his arms crossed against his chest. "Well, go ahead. Take your clothes off and get in."

"You have to leave. I can't take a bath with you here." She nervously twisted the bottom edge of her tee shirt in her hands.

"Come on, Joanie. Just take off your clothes and get in the tub. It's not like I haven't seen it before." Walt chuckled at his own joke.

"No. I don't want you watching me." Horrified, she stood defiantly in front of him.

"If you won't get undressed, I guess I'll have to help you." Walt reached over and grabbed the sides of her tee shirt, forcefully trying to yank it over her head.

"No," she screamed as she pushed his hands away. "I can do it." Walt smiled and lowered his arms. Joanie turned her back to him and slowly pulled off her tee shirt.

"Thatta girl. See? I knew you could do it," he said to her back.

Joanie covered her breasts with her arm while she tried to take off her jeans, one handed. It wasn't working, and she soon realized she had no choice but to use both hands to remove the rest of her clothes. She lowered her arm, feeling embarrassed to be exposed, even though it wasn't anything he hadn't already seen, as he had pointed out. She kept her back to him as she slowly took off the rest of her clothes and left them in a pile on the cold concrete floor.

While keeping her back to her captor, she side-stepped towards the tub, one arm across her breasts and the other hand covering below. She carefully stepped onto the platform and looked into the tub. It was nasty with dirt and stains and had only about six inches of water in the bottom. "I can't take a bath in that," Joanie said.

"You have to. You'll need to get cleaned up at some point. It might as well be now." Walt gave her a gentle pat on her exposed bottom. She turned her head over her shoulder and glared at him before deciding the dirty tub was the lesser of the two evils.

She brought one foot over the edge of the tub. As soon as her toes touched the water, she drew back. "That's freezing! I can't take a bath in cold water!"

"That's water from the garden hose. It's not like it's hooked up to the hot water tank. Now get in there. This is taking too long." Walt grabbed her upper arm from behind and pushed her closer to the tub.

Joanie lowered herself into the tub, drawing a sharp breath as soon as her butt touched the cold water. She tried to turn away from Walt, but the tub was too small to accommodate shifting her position.

She looked around for something to wash with. "There's no soap."

Walt handed her a small, obviously used bar of soap that had been sitting on the platform. She began washing, starting with her arms as discreetly as she could. She didn't dare ask for a washcloth. There was no telling what kind of condition it would be in, if he even had one.

Suddenly, Walt grabbed the hair at the back of her head with one hand and opened the zipper of his pants with the other hand. He pulled out his fully erect member and forced it into her face. She tried to pull away, but he had a tight grasp on her hair, preventing her from moving away from him. His breath came in quick gasps as he gave her instructions on what to do.

She continued to cough and gag until Walt was satisfied.

"Get cleaned up," he said. He turned on his heel and left the bunker.

Joanie, still sitting in the tub, covered her face with her hands and cried. While the tears streamed down her cheeks, she grabbed the soap and scrubbed her face like she had never scrubbed before. She wanted to scrub away the act, the memory, and the shame of what he had done to her. Joanie had learned about intercourse from health class in school, but she had never heard of what he'd just put her through. She was disgusted beyond words.

Finally, with her teeth chattering from the cold, Joanie had no choice but to get out of the tub. She looked around for a towel but didn't see any. In fact, there was nothing she could use to dry off. Her clothes were still in a pile on the floor, just as she had left them what seemed like hours ago, so she wiped off as much water as she could with her hands and put her clothes back on.

Joanie was exhausted, both mentally and physically. Her body hurt. Her brain hurt. She was too tired to cry. Slowly, she made her way back to the mattress and laid down. She curled into the fetal position and wrapped her hands around her waist, as much to warm herself as to feel a sense of comfort.

Although her stomach grumbled loudly, the thought of eating made her even more nauseous. Even so, her eyes gravitated of their own accord to the crate where the plastic container of chicken had been. The cup of water was still there, but the container of food was gone. She would go hungry until he brought her more food, but that was okay. She was numb and had no desire to do anything except sleep.

Later that afternoon, Walt appeared in the bunker with another plastic container, a sleeve of plastic utensils, and a cup of water in his hands. He set them on the milk crate, just as he had done the day before. Joanie watched from the mattress with eyes that seemed to lack emotion.

"I've brought you some beef stew, my Little Flower. I just made it. Well, all I did was open the can and heat it up, but it's good." He reached over to cup her chin with his hand, as if he were a concerned father tending to an unhappy child.

She pulled her chin away from him and stared at the toes of his shoes.

"Now, don't be like that. We're going to be good friends, you and I. You'll see."

Joanie continued to stare at the floor, but she didn't dare speak. If she had spoken to her captor, she would have told him how she hated him. She would have explained how disgusted she was by what he did to her, what he made her do to him. She would have screamed at him, told him how much she missed her family and wanted to go home. Instead, she kept quiet, fighting to keep the words and the tears at bay.

"If you eat your dinner, maybe I'll bring you a present. Doesn't that sound nice?"

He smiled at her, showing teeth that seemed too large for his face.

"Why did you kidnap me?" she asked quietly.

"Well, you see, I am a man, and a man has certain needs." Walt puffed out his chest and put his hands on his hips. "You're here to fulfill those needs, and in exchange, I'll make sure you have everything you need."

"I *need* to go home," Joanie said, with emphasis on the word "need."

"That's not possible. But like I said, I will bring you nice things, and you'll be very comfortable here with me."

"No, I won't be comfortable here. I'll never be happy here. I just want to go home." Joanie could feel the burn behind her eyes as the tears were building. She blinked them back as best she could.

"I'm going to tell you a secret, my Little Flower." He pulled a wallet from the back pocket of his khakis and opened it to expose a shiny silver police badge. "I belong to a very special club. Lots and lots of powerful men belong to this club—very rich men, like politicians, celebrities and even the chief of police, and my job is to teach you all about how to perform sex acts with these men. There are other women like you that help us satisfy our urges, but they live in the house. You need to prove yourself, and someday you'll be able to move to the house, and you'll have a lot more privileges than you have here. But if you don't comply, then your time in this bunker will be extended. And if you cause any problems or fight me about it, someone in your family might get hurt. Someone like little Stevie. That's how it works. Do you understand me?"

Joanie didn't—couldn't—answer him. She was horrified by this revelation. She was to be held as a sex slave for a club of rich and powerful men? Never in her wildest dreams did she ever think this kind of life existed, let alone that she would be dragged into it.

"And don't even think of trying to escape. You see, the door at the end of the tunnel is always locked, and the only way to open it is by dialing the proper code on the padlock. I move it from the outside to the inside, depending on if I'm in here with you or out there in the house with the rest of the girls. That door is always locked, and I'm the only one who knows the code, so if you ever try to leave or hit me over the head with something and knock me out, you still won't be able to escape."

Joanie's chin dropped as she comprehended Walt's words. She would never get out of here, and if she didn't cooperate, her family would be in danger. It was a risk she wasn't willing to take.

Joanie watched Walt's back as he climbed the stepladder and vanished into the tunnel. Her hope for escape disappeared with him.

Little did she know it was all a lie. There was no sex club of powerful men, no one was in the house but Walt, and the badge was one he'd found under a bush years before while he was walking through a local park.

CHAPTER THREE

Over the course of the next several weeks, Joanie became more and more depressed. Walt was raping her on a daily basis, at least once and sometimes twice a day.

She was beside herself with shame, guilt, confusion, and despondency. If only she hadn't been upset with Stevie, Walt wouldn't have seen her crying, and if he hadn't seen her crying, he wouldn't have offered her a ride. If only she had said no to the ride.

Joanie had to force herself not to think about the things Walt was doing to her. She was brought up in a family that didn't talk about things like sex. It just wasn't done. What she knew about the "birds and the bees" she'd learned from health class at school. Even hearing about sex in a classroom filled with other boys and girls was embarrassing to her. Sex with a strange man was, to Joanie, a horrifying and degrading experience.

Becoming pregnant was a concern for the young girl. She tried using a possible pregnancy as a reason to be released. "I can get pregnant, you know," she announced to him.

"You don't have to worry about that. I had a vasectomy years ago."

"What does that mean? What's a vasectomy?" Her cheeks turned bright red from embarrassment as she asked.

"That means I can't have any more kids. I had a procedure done in the doctor's office so I can't make you pregnant. I'm shooting blanks." He laughed, as if he was telling a funny joke.

Unsure whether to believe him, Joanie looked at him out of the corner of her eyes, her eyebrows knit together. She hoped he was telling the truth.

As promised, Walt was bringing objects to Joanie that he called "presents." He referred to them as "fair compensation." One of the first gifts was a wall calendar on which she was told to write the letters B, T, or S within the empty block of each date.

The B represented when she bathed, the T represented when she brushed her teeth, and the S represented when they had sex. The B and T were written on the calendar sporadically, maybe every few days. However, she marked the S every day without exception. Sometimes twice a day.

On the days with a B, she would bathe in just a couple inches of water while he watched. Sometimes, he filmed her with a video camera. That became just one more disgraceful act she was forced to endure. He would even take the soap with him when he left so she couldn't bathe when he wasn't there to watch.

What Walt didn't realize was that Joanie would prefer not to take a bath anyway, since the water from the garden hose was always ice cold. She would never willingly sit in the frigid water. Then, after the bath, it would take a long time to finish drying off and warm up. He never seemed to think of bringing her a towel.

He would also take away the toothbrush and toothpaste after she'd used them, although Joanie wished he would have left them with her. She didn't like the feeling of unbrushed teeth. Ever since she was a little girl, she had taken good care of her teeth and had always taken pride in how they were so white they sparkled.

Regardless of the signifying initials written next to each date, Joanie saw the calendar as nothing more than a sad reminder of how long she had been held captive. Her days were long and lonely, filled with nothing but her own depressing thoughts to occupy her time. She came to think of the bunker as the dungeon.

When Walt was having sex with her, she gradually learned to force her mind to think of something other than what was happening to her. She would stare at the ceiling—if she left her eyes open—and count the cinder blocks. More often, though, she would tightly close her eyes and think of better times.

While he was having sex with her, she refused to think of her family and what they may be doing in her absence. That was just too creepy. Instead, she would think of things like the holidays and how good the house would smell while her mom was cooking. She would try to think about the scent of freshly mown grass or the way the garden looked after her grandmother planted fresh flowers. Occasionally, she would replay scenes in her mind from her favorite television programs—"CSI: Miami" and "Dancing With The Stars."

But when she was alone, she would fondly think about her mother and father, her brother Stevie, and her grandparents. Joanie's father was Native American, her mother was white. Although Joanie's mom loved her father, her mom didn't want to live anywhere else but in the neighborhood where she had grown up. So, from the time Joanie's parents were married, they lived in town and away from the reservation her father had grown up on.

Joanie's paternal grandparents had always lived on the reservation, and she loved visiting them as often as she could. Joanie enjoyed learning about their culture from both her grandmother and her grandfather, who took pride in showing her the Native ways. Preserving their culture was important to them all.

Her grandmother was a clan mother, highly respected among their people. She was especially knowledgeable about the local herbs and their uses.

Some herbs were used medicinally while others were used in cooking. Before Joanie was kidnapped, her grandmother had been teaching her how to cook with the herbs and vegetables they were growing in the garden behind her grandparent's house. Joanie was proud of this season's batch of what was known to their tribe as "the three sisters"—beans, corn and squash. Her grandmother instilled in her the importance of lovingly planting, tending, and harvesting these plants. She called it "from seed to table." They spent many hours together, with her grandmother as the teacher and Joanie as the student.

Some of Joanie's favorite times were when she and her grandmother would gather a variety of nuts and berries, mustard greens, and dandelions from the land on the reservation. Then they would go back to her grandmother's kitchen and spend many hours either hanging the herbs to dry for use during the wintertime or using them right away in a delicious dish for dinner or dessert.

Her grandfather was the hunter and fisherman of the family, and although Stevie was still a bit young to learn how to hunt, their grandfather had been showing him how to fish. Joanie had a picture on her dresser at home of her grandfather and her brother standing together with their backs to the camera as they quietly fished in the lake near their grandparents' home. Her grandmother had taken the picture at sunset, with a sky beautifully colored in oranges, reds and yellows, and was one of Joanie's favorites.

Keeping those memories alive in her mind was important to Joanie. It gave her a reason to look to the future, to the day when she would get away from Walt.

One afternoon, Walt entered the dungeon with a cold fast-food hamburger and fries on a Styrofoam plate in one hand and a Bible in the other. Joanie was sitting in the room with the mattress, her back resting in the corner, as she usually did.

"I've been remiss, my Little Flower, in not keeping up with your religious education." He sat down in a lawn chair he'd dragged from the other room and placed it near the mattress. "I've brought you a Bible so we can read from it every day. Would you like that?"

"No. I don't practice the same religion as you do. I'm Native American," she said.

"Don't you believe in God?" Walt gave her a puzzled look.

"Yes, I believe in god, but our god is called the Great Spirit. We also believe in other gods, like the god of goodness and light and the god of evil. There's also Mother Earth."

"It sounds to me," said Walt, "like you need to learn about the *right* god. All those gods you believe in are bullshit. Even the very first of the ten commandments says, 'You shall have no other gods before me.' That means there's only one god. Everyone knows that."

She was entirely at his mercy for every facet of her current life, so she tried not to irritate him. Still, when he started bad-mouthing her religion, it hit a nerve.

"That's the god you worship. Not mine." Joanie was firm with Walt, something she usually didn't have the energy to do.

Ignoring her, Walt opened his Bible to the first page and began reading out loud.

Joanie knew fighting Walt would be a waste of time. She also knew that to him she was no more than a puppet on a string. She ate what he brought her, she bathed and brushed her teeth when he told her to, and her only forms of entertainment were a small radio that only seemed to be able to tune into scratchy stations and the outdated Reader's Digest magazines he brought her once in a while.

She tried to listen to the radio occasionally, but it was difficult to get a good reception in the underground bunker/dungeon. It was more static than music, but once in a while, the FM station was clear enough that she could hum along to the tune.

She interrupted his Bible reading. "You need to let me go. I don't want to stay here anymore. Please let me go home," she begged for what seemed like the thousandth time.

"Don't you remember what I told you about the rich and powerful people I work with? Even if *I* wanted to let you go, *they* would never allow you to go. You've learned so much since you've been here. As a matter of fact, I was talking to the police chief just the other day. I told him how good you are at what you do. He's eager to see for himself, but I told him you weren't quite ready yet. You need just a bit more practice."

With that, Walt threw the Bible aside and stood up. Joanie's eyes glazed over, knowing what would happen next.

After Joanie had been in the dungeon for about a month, Walt brought her a notebook, similar to the kind she'd used in school. He handed her a pen and said, "I thought you might like to write a note to your parents and tell them you're okay."

For the first time since she'd been kidnapped, Joanie's spirits lifted, but her optimism was short-lived.

"Here's what I want you to say. Tell them you're staying with friends and that you're doing fine."

"But that's not true!" protested Joanie. "I'm not with friends, and I sure as hell am not fine! What is wrong with you? Can't you see this is just plain wrong?"

"I have no control over the situation. The men that are far more powerful than me want us to keep practicing for a bit longer, then you might be able to move to the house with the rest of the girls. Come on. Let's write the note, and I promise I'll mail it."

"Do you promise?" Joanie asked dubiously.

"Yes, I do. I promise I'll mail it." With his finger, Walt made an X over his heart.

Joanie took the pen and paper and eagerly began to write, "Dear Mom, Dad, and Stevie." Without warning, Walt ripped the notebook from her lap. He read the small bit that Joanie had written.

"That part is okay, but I want you to write what I tell you to write. If you want me to mail the letter, you'll write exactly what I say." He gave her back the notebook and proceeded to dictate the letter. He told her to let her parents know she was in good health and was staying with friends but not reveal where she was. It was an ambiguous note, but at least it was a note. And they would recognize her handwriting and know she wasn't dead.

The next day, he told Joanie he mailed the letter. She would eventually learn that to be true.

CHAPTER FOUR

As time went on, Joanie became more and more depressed, eventually giving up hope she'd ever be released. Walt continued to use threats to her family as a tool, holding it over her head that he could hurt them or even kill them if she didn't cooperate with his demands.

Thinking about being reunited with her family became too painful. Joanie resorted to writing poems in her head but gave that up when they became nothing more than depressing wishes for death. She picked at her fingernails until they bled. She stopped thinking about her heritage, instead counting the microscopic holes in the concrete. Her once-beautiful hair went from greasy to stringy to dry and brittle. Her skin became blotchy and oily.

The calendar was her only indication of the passage of time, but with no natural light, the hour of the day meant nothing. Only Walt's reference to the food he brought as breakfast, lunch, or dinner let her know if it was morning, noon, or night.

He brought her food, usually once a day, although it was never on a regular schedule and wasn't enough to fill her empty belly. She bathed and brushed her teeth, only when he allowed her to. When she took a bath, the water drained from the tub and pooled on the floor in a puddle that never seemed to go away. There was no drain in the cement floor for the water to be piped to the outside. It would take days for the water to evaporate, and by then, the bunker would be damp, moldy, and smelly.

Walt had taken to calling her his "Little Rose" because, according to him, she'd become precious to him and the rose was the most precious flower of all.

If he only knew how much she hated that nickname, how much she hated him.

Joanie had been with Walt for about three months when he brought her another present. With a wide grin, he handed her a photo showing the inside of her home, her mother standing at the stove. Her back was to the camera, but it was clearly her mother, wearing her favorite sweater. The next photo was of Stevie sitting on the couch in the living room, watching television. The last photo was of her father washing the car in the driveway.

Joanie felt the blood drain from her face, her vision growing dark. She looked from the photos to Walt and back to the photos.

"Oh, my god," she whispered. "How did you get these pictures?"

"Very simple. I rang the doorbell, and when your mom came to the door, I said I was there to check the status of the house on behalf of the landlord. I told her I was looking for damages and leaky pipes. She bought it hook, line, and sinker." Walt laughed as if someone had just told him a funny joke.

Joanie was speechless. This confirmed his threats, that he remembered where her family lived, and he could hurt them at any time. She had lost hope long ago of ever escaping, but now she knew she was justified in feeling afraid, not for herself, but for her family. She hadn't thought the nightmare she was living could get any worse... until then.

With a sick laugh and a sadistic smile curling his lips, Walt grabbed at Joanie and proceeded with the daily ritual of sex. This time, it seemed he was even more forceful than normal, as if the photos had given him a stronger, more intense sense of empowerment.

As he lay on top of her, she turned her head to the side to focus on the photos she still gripped tightly in her hand. She had always been fearful of the threats he made against her family, but she prayed he would leave them alone. She thought him crazy, but she hoped he wasn't dangerous enough to kill. The photos changed everything.

When he finished, he headed towards the stepladder but turned to look at her.

"You're so good at sex, my Little Rose. You've learned so much about how to please a man. I enjoy the times when we are together."

A single tear ran down her cheek as she curled up on the mattress and hugged the photos of her family to her chest. She fell asleep wondering if she would ever see them again.

As the weeks dragged on, Walt continued to shower Joanie with what he called gifts. Sometimes he would bring her a cookie or candy bar, but usually it was another outdated magazine. Still, she would read them slowly, making them last. There was no point in rushing through them.

He even started bringing her some clothes. She had lost weight, and the clothes she had been wearing when he kidnapped her no longer fit. The new clothes were obviously from Goodwill, but she wasn't complaining. Anything that would keep her warm and covered in the chilly dampness of the dungeon was a plus.

The routine never changed much—she endured daily rapes and Bible readings, occasional baths and brushing her teeth. When Walt wasn't with her, she entertained herself by reading the magazines he brought and listening to the radio when static didn't interfere. She'd read the magazines so many times the pages were committed to memory.

Listening to the radio was something that broke up her day. It not only filled the empty, silent void of being alone, Joanie could also hear what was happening in the outside world. Every hour, the radio station would broadcast the news headlines and the weather. As a young kid, the news was never something she cared about, but now it became a godsend and her only connection to the world beyond the dungeon. Still, as the broadcaster spoke of current events, it became yet another reminder that life outside the bunker was moving on without her.

Joanie gave in to dark thoughts and gave up. Depression and anger were her constant companions. Her emotions would come in waves, similar to the stages of grief. When depressed, thoughts of life beyond the dungeon became painful. When she was in denial, the tears were non-stop, leaving her exhausted, her face feeling dry and tight. Anger, something she rarely experienced, found its way into her heart and she shouted at Walt, demanding to be released. During those times, he let her know he was in charge. She would be released if and when he decided.

The one thing she never expected was that Walt's attention towards her changed. He still called her his "Little Rose" or "Precious Rose," but he also referred to her as his girlfriend.

"How can I be your girlfriend if you're so much older than I am? We don't go out on dates, either," she observed.

Walt ignored the comment about their ages. "Just because I don't take you to the movies, it doesn't mean we still can't be boyfriend and girlfriend. Besides, if you leave the safety of the bunker, the police chief will think you're ready to join the other women in the house. I'd rather keep you all to myself. I don't want to share your special abilities with anyone else. You're much safer here."

CHAPTER FIVE

One day blended into the next, the routines the same from day to day and month to month. A Christmas passed and then another, marked only by the letters on her calendar. Birthdays passed without a cake or a card. In the bunker, summers were cold, the winters more so.

Joanie had developed a resigned indifference to being held captive, her thoughts rarely turning towards escape. Rather, she considered death as being the only way out of the dungeon.

According to the daily calendar on which she continued to write an S, B or T, Joanie had been held captive for over two years and was now seventeen years old.

Walt had continually made threats against her parents and brother in order to keep her submissive. Joanie had heard it so many times, it became nothing more than an ear worm as if it were an annoying song playing incessantly in her mind. She believed him, she wanted to yell at him. She just got tired of the constant reminders.

One day, several months later, Walt came into the dungeon and said, "I have a surprise for you, my Precious Rose, and you're going to love it. I have some business to conduct in California, and I'm taking you with me."

"Are you serious?" Joanie was dumbfounded by the news. He was letting her out?

"I would only be gone for a few days, but I can't leave you here by yourself. And if I ask someone else to bring your food every day, they might touch you the way I do, and I can't allow that to happen. Besides, I need our togetherness every day, so if you come with me, we can still have our fun."

Joanie's mind was spinning. She had never been out of the area before because her family had never taken a vacation, although they had occasionally visited the local zoo when she and Stevie were small. Even then, the zoo was only a few miles from her home, so it wasn't like they had traveled a long way to get there.

Going to California sounded like an opportunity she'd never have again, but the fact it was with Walt took the excitement out of it.

The idea of getting out of the dungeon was enticing, but could she trust his word that they were really going to California? Was this a ruse to take her somewhere and kill her to be rid of her? Maybe she should refuse to go. Starving to death in the dungeon would be better than getting killed, her body dumped somewhere where no one would ever find her.

But realizing she had no choice, she would have to take her chances and hope he didn't kill her or worse, kill someone in her family. She would accept him at his word and go with him to California, as he demanded.

While he had sex with her, Joanie's mind ran through various scenarios. He had said it would only be a couple days, so they must be flying to California. Although she'd never been to one, she had seen airports on television, and they seemed to be very busy with lots of people carrying large bags of luggage. Maybe she could get lost in the crowd and run away from Walt. If there was an opportunity, she decided, she would try to escape.

The next morning, Walt appeared at her bedside while she was still asleep. He poked her on the shoulder. "Come on, my Precious Rose. We have a big day ahead of us."

"What's going on?" Joanie tried to blink the sleep from her eyes.

"I told you. We're going to California."

"I didn't know you meant today. We're going today?" She was still half asleep.

"Yes. Come on, now. We need to get ready, then we'll go to the airport." Walt reached for his belt buckle. "It's going to be a long day, so you're going to give me a little loving right now. There won't be time later."

When he was satisfied, he instructed her to get in the tub—still with only a few inches of water—and then told her to get dressed and brush her teeth.

"How long are we going for?" she asked. "I don't have anything to wear, and I'm going to need clothes."

"I've already taken care of that," he said as he pointed to a small suitcase near the ladder. "I've already put some new clothes in there for you and me, plus toothbrushes for both of us, and a new hairbrush for you. I want you to look your best."

Joanie looked at him quizzically. She still didn't trust him. "Why? Why are we going to California?"

"I told you, I've got business to conduct. Now, come on. Let's go." Walt grabbed the luggage with one hand, her arm with the other, and pulled her towards the ladder. "And don't try anything funny. You know what will happen if you do."

A shiver crawled up Joanie's spine as Walt's ever-present threat sunk in. She felt torn between the excitement of escaping the dungeon and the fear he might kill her. If they truly were going to California and she managed to escape, would he try to kill a member of her family? She couldn't bear the thought of someone in her family getting hurt or killed because of her.

With Walt right behind her, she crawled through the tunnel and came out in the small closet-sized area that was between the two doors. The door leading into the basement was locked, just as she had found out long ago that it would be. In all this time, she had only dared the one time when she was first kidnapped, to enter the tunnel on her own to see if he was locking her in.

He reached past her to the padlock above the doorknob and dialed the code, shielding the combination from her eyes with his other hand. He opened the door and placed the padlock on the opposite side. They made their way through the next door that was fronted by the empty shelving unit and into the basement. It was all just as Joanie remembered.

As they walked through the basement, Joanie looked around at the multitude of overflowing shelves and noticed it had become even more cluttered and filthy in the two years since she had been brought here.

They walked silently through the kitchen and into the living room. The rooms were full of papers, bottles and cans—she remembered it had been just as messy on that horrible first day.

As Joanie gazed around the living room, her eyes settled on a strange man sitting in an armchair. Her heart began to race and sweat formed on her brow as she recalled Walt's warnings that powerful men were waiting to rape her. She stared at him. He stared at her, neither one saying a word.

Walt spoke first. "Joanie, this is my son, Gregory. He's taking us to the airport."

Joanie could hear her heart pounding in her ears. Gregory stared at her and, without breaking eye contact, asked, "Who the hell is she?"

"I've been taking care of her. She has an eating disorder, so I'm helping to coach her," Walt lied.

The man, Gregory, looked through squinted eyes at Walt. After several seconds, his focus returned to Joanie. He stared at her but didn't speak. Finally, he stood up and said, "Let's go."

As Gregory walked out the front door, Walt put his arm out in front of Joanie, stopping her in her tracks. He pulled a dark bandana from his back pocket. "You need to put this on before we go."

"What are you talking about?" Joanie looked from his arm across her chest to the navy-blue bandana he held in front of her.

"Turn around so I can tie it."

Joanie hesitated, but did as he asked, thinking it was a strange thing to wear around her neck. It wasn't until he pulled it over her eyes that she flinched away from him.

"What are you doing? Get that off me!" Panicked, she tried swiping at the material to clear her eyes, but he was holding onto it too tightly.

Walt yanked at the ends of the bandana gathered at the back of her head and tried to tie it into a knot. She kept trying to pull away from him. As he pulled on the bandana, a few strands of hair got caught in the knot and were painfully yanked out of her head.

"Stop!" he yelled. Instinctively, she rested her hands at her sides.

"Why are you doing this? Why are you putting this thing over my eyes?" she asked.

"It's best that you don't see where we are. You don't need to know where I live. This is just to protect the other girls who live here and the men who come to see them."

Joanie hadn't been blindfolded when he'd first brought her to the dungeon, but perhaps he'd forgotten. It didn't matter. She had no idea where they were, anyway. At the time of her abduction, she and her family were fairly new to the area.

After years of living a horrifying life in Walt's dungeon, Joanie knew there was nothing she could say that could possibly change his mind, so she let him lead her blindly outside to the car. He gently turned her around and instructed her to sit. Her butt caught the edge of the seat, so she swung her feet around until she was entirely in the back seat of the vehicle. Her car door slammed shut, followed by another door being slammed. She felt the car begin to move.

Walt and his son Gregory carried on a conversation, but they each spoke softly enough that she couldn't make out the words. From the tone, it sounded like an argument, but about what, she didn't know. The radio was up too loud, the speakers blaring from behind her, for her to make out their words.

Joanie found herself enjoying the radio more than the conversation in the front seat. It was nice to hear songs that were not full of static and, as a result, hard to understand. She felt tempted to hum along but decided against it. She didn't want Walt or his son to misunderstand her happiness, fleeting as it might be.

Finally, after what she figured to be twenty or thirty minutes, the car came to a stop, and Gregory turned it off. She heard someone open one of the front seat doors, then felt the sudden rush of air as someone opened her door. Without warning, someone ripped the bandana from her eyes, taking more hair with it. Joanie blinked at the sudden burst of sunshine and tried to focus. It had been a very long time since she had seen the sunshine.

She stepped out of the car and looked around. Her eyes began to water as they adjusted to the bright sunlight. She blinked away the tears and saw they were in a parking lot.

A jet flew loudly over their heads. Joanie felt like she could reach out and touch it, it flew so closely. They were obviously at the airport.

Walt reached into the back seat of the car and grabbed their one shared piece of luggage. "Thanks for the ride, Son. I've got it from here." He reached for Joanie's elbow and led her towards a large building where people were rushing in and out through the doors. Most seemed to be pulling carts loaded with piles of luggage, while others carried one or two bags with their hands. She looked behind and saw Gregory still sitting in the car, staring at her.

Suddenly, Walt yanked her arm, bringing her gaze forward again. "Listen to me. I want you to remember that I know a lot of people. A lot of important people. If you try to run or try to bring attention to yourself, you'll be in a lot of trouble. Your family, too, might be in trouble. Got me?"

"Y-yes, I understand. I'll behave." Joanie had never been in an airport before, and she realized that even if she could run away from Walt, she had no idea where to run to. So many people were going in so many different directions, it was impossible for her to figure out the direction that would lead to her escape.

Even if she found a way to secretly ask someone for help, she couldn't take the chance of that person being a friend of Walt's. He had threatened her family many, many times, and Joanie loved them too much to put them in harm's way.

Awed by the sights and sounds of the airport, Joanie let Walt lead her to the boarding gate. Once there, he pulled two tickets out of his jacket pocket and gave them to the smiling woman behind the counter. She scanned them, keyed something into her computer, and gave them back to Walt.

"Thank you so much," he said with a large, toothy smile to the woman. "Have a nice day." Grabbing Joanie firmly by the elbow, he lead the way past the woman at the counter and through the terminal. After several minutes, they joined the line of people waiting to board the plane. No one looked at the young woman and the man who had a firm grasp of her elbow.

Finally, they reached the large jetway that led to the waiting plane. Alarmed, Joanie stopped just before entering it. "No! No, I can't go in there!"

"What's your problem?" he asked, gritting his teeth. "Get in there."

With eyes the size of saucers, Joanie looked between the jetway and Walt, back and forth, as if her head were on a swivel. The jetway leading to the plane looked too much like the tunnel that led to the dungeon. "I can't go in there! I'll never get out again!"

Walt pushed her to the side, the line of passengers behind them giving them strange looks as they waited to board. "What are you talking about? That leads to the plane," he hissed, as he shook her arm.

"It does? Are you sure it goes to the plane?" she asked nervously. She watched as the passengers filed past her and Walt and entered the strange metal tunnel. None of the passengers were coming back their way.

"Of course. How else would we get to the plane? Now knock it off before I have to call a friend and have them deal with you."

Joanie hesitated, letting his words sink in, her breath coming in quick gasps. "Okay. Okay. I'm okay."

"I sure as hell hope so. If you do that again, I'll call my friend the assemblyman to come pick you up. He works right down the road. And I'll go on to California by myself."

"No, please don't call him. I'll be good. I promise." Joanie hung her head, trying to calm her breathing.

Walt led her onto the plane and into their seats. She watched as he stowed their one piece of baggage in a cabinet over their heads. After a few minutes, the plane moved to the runway.

She gripped the armrests tightly as the plane lifted off, rose steeply, then banked to the side in a sharp pitch. Once the plane leveled off, she relaxed a bit. She looked around at the other passengers, who settled into their seats with ear buds, books, and pillows for napping.

It was a long flight to California, but Joanie surprised herself by enjoying it. She had the window seat and gazed through the thick glass as they flew through the puffy white clouds that looked like cotton balls. Every once in a while, the clouds separated long enough for her to see the ground below, with cities, roads and farmland everywhere she looked. The scenery below resembled a patchwork quilt. It was incredible!

About an hour into the flight, a movie called *Marley and Me* began playing on small screens that hung from the ceiling of the plane. The passengers listened to the movie with earphones that were plugged into the armrests. It wasn't until then that Joanie realized how much she missed going to the movies with her friends. Her eyes began to water at the memories, but she bit her bottom lip to stop the emotions. She didn't want Walt to see her getting teary-eyed.

Once they arrived in California, they grabbed a taxi that brought them to their hotel. Walt signed them in at the front desk, and they found their room. Joanie watched as Walt used something that looked like a credit card and slipped it into a square box above the doorknob. She heard the click of the door being unlocked.

Once in the room, Joanie looked around in amazement. The room was impressive, with two enormous beds covered in matching quilts, a shiny wooden dresser, and a flat-screen television. She was surprised to see a coffeepot with cellophane-wrapped mugs, packets of instant coffee, cream and sugar sitting on the dresser. That was something she'd always seen in the kitchen, not a bedroom.

She threw open the draperies to check out the view, which turned out to be the parking lot. Still, after more than two years of living in the dungeon, it was a beautiful sight.

Then she climbed onto one of the two beds, stretched out, and claimed that one for herself. Walt ignored her comment.

She found the remote for the television on the nightstand and spent the next few minutes exploring the channels and shows. She'd forgotten how much she used to enjoy TV.

"I'm too tired to go to the restaurant downstairs. Let's order room service instead," Walt said. In truth, it wasn't that he was too tired, but rather, he wanted to keep Joanie close to his side and away from prying eyes. If they stayed in the room, their chances of drawing attention to themselves were minimal.

Joanie had never stayed in a hotel before. She'd heard of room service but never experienced it for herself. Eating in bed? What would her parents think? The thought of her parents stopped her cold, but Joanie shook it off. She didn't want to be sad now. The little bit of freedom mixed with the new things she was experiencing were amazing.

While they waited for their cheeseburgers to be delivered, Walt climbed into bed with Joanie. She had been watching television and was leaning against the headrest, totally engrossed in the shows she hadn't seen in almost three years.

He wrapped his arm around her shoulders and gave her a squeeze. She tensed, her concentration on the television interrupted.

"Don't be so frigid." He laughed. "We can't do anything now. They'll be here in a few minutes with our burgers."

Joanie relaxed a bit under his touch, knowing she wouldn't have to have sex with him, but the happiness she'd felt after the day of freedom and adventure was gone. She might not have been in the dungeon, but she was still his prisoner, still at his mercy.

The next morning, Joanie woke up to Walt's arm wrapped around her waist, his hand reaching under her panties. She closed her eyes, pretending to still be asleep, but it didn't matter to him. He would have her, no matter what.

"We need to take a shower," he said when he was done with her. "Let's go."

He walked Joanie into the bathroom and closed the door behind them. "I'm not letting you out of my sight. We'll take a shower together."

In the days before her kidnapping, Joanie would have been mortified at the suggestion of two people showering together, but after all that time with Walt, she had lost all sense of privacy. He'd taken her innocence, her dignity, and her pride. There was nothing left to lose. He turned on the water and climbed into the tub right behind her.

It was the first time in over two years that she'd been in a shower, and she reveled in it. The warm water running over her hair and shoulders was a welcome sensation. If she had her way, she'd stay there all morning. It felt wonderful, at least it did, until Walt began rubbing the soap on her back.

"I'll order breakfast, and have it delivered to the room again," Walt said after they'd both dressed. In a few minutes, they were enjoying French toast, bacon, orange juice, and coffee.

Between the burgers the night before and the breakfast that morning, Joanie couldn't remember the last time she'd tasted anything so delicious. It sure beat the cold leftovers Walt had been bringing her for such a long time.

When they finished eating, Walt looked at his watch and announced it was time to go. He began putting what few items they had in the luggage.

"Where are we going?" Joanie asked. She knew it would be "we" not "you."

"I bought some land a while back, so I need to sign some papers. After that, we'll be going home." Joanie felt a wave of disappointment wash over her when she heard Walt say they would be going home so soon. The thought of going back to the dungeon was heartbreaking. She pushed it out of her mind, determined to enjoy the last few hours of freedom, sunshine and the sights, before she'd be forced back into the dark, dank, smelly, moldy, musty, showerless, and lonely dungeon.

Walt returned their room key to a man at the front counter and settled the bill. As they left the hotel, Walt flagged down an available taxi in front of the building. He gave the driver an address as the cab pulled away from the curb.

The taxi stopped in front of a very tall, red brick building with dark windows that seemed to reach the sky. As they got out of the taxi, Joanie stopped and stood still on the sidewalk, forcing people to walk around her. She was staring at the door. One by one, individuals walked into one of the glass partitions that made up the door and pushed on the glass until they were on the other side. They made it look easy. She looked at Walt, who was smiling at her.

"Haven't you ever gone through a revolving door? Come on, it's easy, but you have to be quick. Just jump in." Joanie did as Walt suggested, but she ended up going around twice before getting the timing right and stepping into the large marble foyer.

"That was cool!" she said, her eyes shining in delight. Walt laughed at her response.

He approached the young receptionist sitting at the desk in the middle of the foyer. Joanie noticed that Walt was pouring on the charm as he talked to her. He was asking where he could find the lawyer's office. The receptionist seemed impervious to his flirting and told them they would find the office on the fifteenth floor. With a smile that did not reach her eyes, she dismissed Walt by returning her sight to her computer.

They were the only two in the elevator, so Walt took the opportunity to make sure Joanie understood she was to remain quiet and not say a word. "This is man's business. You need to just sit quietly. I don't want you uttering a peep. Do you understand?"

"Yes, sir. I understand." Joanie hung her head.

Joanie kept her promise and only spoke when spoken to. She didn't even correct Walt when he introduced her to the attorney as his niece. Instead, she offered a short, "Hello."

Once the paperwork was signed, Walt hailed another taxi, and they drove to the airport.

"We have an hour to kill before we board the plane. Let's get something to eat."

They found a bar that offered food and sat at the counter. Joanie chose a grilled cheese sandwich and a soda. Walt opted for a cheeseburger and a beer.

It was another long ride on the plane to get home. Joanie and Walt both slept for a few hours, but before she knew it, they were landing. Her stomach tightened at the thoughts of returning to the dungeon now that their trip was over.

A crowd of people were rushing back and forth on their way to wherever they were going, so Walt had a tight grip on Joanie's arm. He hesitated, just before the doors leading to the outside, and pulled Joanie aside, out of the way of the throng of people.

"Listen, Joanie. You're very special to me, and I enjoyed everything about our special time together, but it's time you went home to your parents and Stevie."

Joanie couldn't believe her ears. Did she hear him right? He was letting her go?

The words wouldn't come, her mouth opening and closing like a fish out of water. A torrent of tears fell down her cheeks. After several moments, she finally found her voice. "What? Are you serious? I can go home?"

"Yeah, you can go home. I've told you before, I'm in control. I decide when you can leave and it's time you left, but you'll need to call your folks for a ride." He took two quarters out of his pocket and pressed them into her hand. She looked through the tears at the coins in the palm of her hand. She gripped them tightly with her fingertips, afraid they might disappear. By the time she looked up, he had walked away.

Joanie frantically looked around for the nearest pay phone. She found one not too far away, hanging on the wall of the terminal. Thankfully, her parents' phone number hadn't changed, and she was able to call them, to tell them she wanted to come home. Her mother, father, and Stevie were there to pick her up within minutes.

With many tears and hugs, their reunion took place on the sidewalk in front of the terminal. Travelers walked around them, some smiling at the happiness they displayed, others frowning at the inconvenience.

Finally, Joanie was driven home, her parents in the front seat of the family car, she and Stevie holding hands in the back seat. Through teary eyes, she looked out the windows, getting a newfound appreciation for her surroundings.

When her parents asked her where she had been all this time, she couldn't bear the thought that her family might look at her with disgust, humiliation, and shame, knowing she had endured continual rape for almost three years. She opened her mouth to say something, but she couldn't form the words. She looked into her brother's eyes and her parents' expectant faces. The shame and disgust of every act, every humiliating experience, washed over her like the slimy, dirty water of her so-called baths. What would they think of her? What did she think of herself? She had done so much to save them from Walt's threats every single day. She needed to save them from the horror she'd experienced, the filth that would never wash away. And so, she did something she'd never done before. She lied. She lied to her mother. She lied to her father. She lied to her precious little brother. Joanie stuck to the same story Walt had forced her to write in the letter she'd written to them after her first month of captivity. Just as in that letter, she said, "I was staying with friends."

Her mother admitted that they'd received her letter, but the family hadn't believed what she'd written because it didn't make sense that Joanie would run away to a friend's house and not tell them anything about it.

That's when Joanie learned that Walt had indeed mailed the letter as promised. She had often wondered if he had.

Her mother kept asking why she hadn't called them, or at the very least, why didn't she send another letter? She admitted to being hurt that Joanie had left with no explanation.

Joanie refused to elaborate or say anything more detailed than that. She felt guilty because she knew her mother was hurt. Joanie hated lying to her family, but she figured there were things that were best left unsaid.

Joanie grappled with the idea of going to the authorities to report her kidnapping and continuous, daily rapes and sexual assaults. She dismissed that idea. No way could she relive the horror of the dungeon and tell someone what had happened, even if that person was a police officer. If she couldn't tell her family, she certainly couldn't tell a total stranger what Walt had forced her to do.

Besides, she'd promised Walt time and time again that if he let her go, she wouldn't tell, although it was not out of respect for him that she stayed silent. It was out of fear. It was fear of Walt's threats and his powerful friends.

For a very long time, Joanie kept her promise to Walt and did not tell anyone about him, the bunker/dungeon, or what he'd forced her to go through. Joanie Deerhunter would keep that promise for a dozen years.

CHAPTER SIX

Walter Pyke had a serious problem. He craved sex on a regular—specifically, a daily—basis. It would be easy to pick up a hooker or even a willing bar patron, but he didn't like having to pay for sex, and sometimes the women he found in the bars wanted a boyfriend, while all he wanted was sex, and lots of it.

He also preferred having a woman accessible at a moment's notice. When the mood struck, so to speak. He had a healthy sex drive, which he maintained by eating the little blue pills like candy.

When he had held Joanie Deerhunter in the dungeon, it had worked out perfectly. He took good care of her, believing he was giving her everything she needed, and all he asked in return was to have sex every day. Sometimes twice a day.

While Joanie was in the bunker, she had become so depressed, so passive, that sex for Walter had become nothing more than a daily ritual done without thought or emotion. He wanted more than that. Sex in and of itself is great, but he would rather have sex with feelings. Even when she fought with him, at least it was showing something, that she wasn't just the shell of a person. As a result, he thought long and hard about releasing her but decided that having sex with someone who just laid there was still better than no sex at all. He would keep her for a bit longer.

The decision to release Joanie came after Gregory had driven them to the airport. Walt was pretty sure Gregory didn't believe the story that he was counseling Joanie about her eating habits. They had argued on the way to the airport and Gregory had threatened to go to the cops. Walt wasn't concerned about the cops. He figured since he took good care of Joanie by giving her food, water, and a make-shift bathroom, they couldn't arrest him for anything. Still, he didn't want the authorities or anyone else to know about the bunker.

Since Gregory hadn't been in the bunker since he was a kid, Walt didn't think his son would remember the bunker after all these years. He doubted Gregory would even think of it. Regardless, he decided it just wasn't worth taking the chance on having anyone getting into his private business, son or otherwise. That's when Walt realized he would have to let Joanie go. The perfect time, he'd decided, would be on the way back from California, and that's exactly what he did.

Walt had released Joanie four years prior and still missed having her around. Maybe he should think about having another female in the dungeon for a while. Yes, that would be a good idea. After all, a man had urges, and he believed women were put on this earth to satisfy those urges.

He'd start looking tomorrow for another woman to fill his needs.

Walt headed into town the next morning to search for a woman. On the way, he also looked for bottles and cans. He had an enormous collection of bottles and cans stored in the basement but was always looking for more. Some he kept, but most he turned in for the nickel deposit. After a while, those nickels added up.

He had a dozen or more shelving units in his basement loaded with various bottles and cans, the ones he'd saved. At last count, he had about 11,000 of them stored on the shelves. Someday, he should probably begin taking them to the recycling center, but they were special. Most were different kinds of imported beer, and he enjoyed collecting the different labels. He had even purchased some on eBay.

He had a hard time getting rid of things. His wife, before she passed away, used to call him a hoarder. If she could see the house now, she would not be happy. He had kept mountains of bills, receipts, newspapers, and magazines. He figured he might need one of the receipts someday to see how much he paid for something, or if he remembered a magazine article he'd read, he might want to re-read it. No, it was not a good idea to throw anything away.

Walt drove slowly through the neighborhoods, looking for women and discarded cans. Occasionally, he would spot a woman, but either she was with someone, or she didn't appear to be someone he would be interested in. He needed to find a woman by herself that he found attractive, and he could easily grab.

Walt was getting hungry and decided to look down one last street before he turned towards home for lunch. He'd already collected about fifteen bottles and cans. Not bad for a couple hours of searching.

While looking for beverage containers on the side of the road, he saw a girl sitting on the curb, leaning against a "No Parking" sign with her legs stretched out in front of her. She was by herself. He slowed down to get a good look at her. She appeared to be about seventeen, maybe eighteen years old, although she had her head down, so he couldn't tell for sure. Her long, black hair covered her face.

He quickly circled the block and came back to the girl. She was still at the curb, still with her head resting on her chest. From what he could tell by the way she filled out her shirt, it was a nice chest.

He slowed down and pulled up next to her. He called to her, but she didn't answer. With a sly grin on his face, he got out of the car and walked towards her. "Excuse me," he said. "Can you help me?"

She still didn't acknowledge him. "Excuse me, miss?" He poked her shoulder with his finger. He looked to the left and right, but the few people on the sidewalk weren't paying attention to him or the girl.

After a couple more jabs to her shoulder, she slowly lifted her head and looked at him. He could tell from her heavy eyelids and the smell of cheap booze that surrounded her, she was drunk.

"Can you help me?" he asked again.

"What do you want?" She blinked her eyes as if she were fighting to stay awake.

"How'd you like to earn $20?" he asked her.

"Sure. What do I have to do?" She lifted her hand to shield her eyes from the noon sun.

"I need you to deliver a package to someone. I'll drive you there. You just have to give it to them."

"That's it?" she slurred. "Just give someone a package?"

"Yep. That's it. Do that, and I'll give you a $20 bill." He gave her a smile.

"Sure, I can do that. Let's go." She attempted to stand up but leaned too far forward. Walt caught her, just before she fell face-first into the road.

"Whoa, there, young lady. Take it easy." He grabbed her by the shoulders to steady her, but not before his hand brushed against her breast. She was too drunk to realize what he'd done.

Walt helped her into the front seat and fastened her seatbelt for her. He copped another feel as the latch clicked into place.

She appeared to be waking up a bit on the ride back to Walt's house. "So, what are we doing?" she asked.

"I want you to deliver a package for me, remember?" he said.

"Oh, yeah. Where's this package?" She was looking out the window, as if the answer was there. "And where's the money?"

"The package is at my house. I didn't bring it with me, but I'll give you the money once you deliver the package."

"Okay. That's cool." She rested her chin on her chest, and in a few moments, Walt heard light snoring. She had fallen asleep.

He pulled in the driveway, and as he stopped in front of his house, Walt shook her shoulder. "Hey, wake up. We're here."

She lifted her head and looked out the windows. "Where are we?" she asked.

"At my house. Come on, let's get that package." Walt exited the car, hurried to the other side, and opened the car door for her. Once she was able to stand, he led her into the house and down the hall towards the garage. "What's your name, anyway?"

"My name is Gabrielle Reyes. What's yours?"

"My name is Walter, but you can call me Walt." He gave her a wide smile, hoping to look friendly.

Walt led Gabrielle through the garage and down the steps into the basement.

Gabrielle stopped at the base of the steps and looked at the rows and rows of shelves filled with bottles and cans. "Wait a minute," she said. "Where is this package?"

"It's in here. I have it in a secret hiding place. We just have to get to the other side of the basement, and I can show you."

Gabrielle looked at him out of the corner of her eyes. The buzz was beginning to wear off, and she was slowly coming to her senses. "You better not be bullshitting me."

"No, I'm telling the truth. I have a package for you, hidden behind a shelf at the other end of the basement." He looked at her wide-eyed and nodded his head, trying to look sincere, as if to prove he wasn't lying.

He led the way, with Gabrielle following. When he stopped at the shelving unit resting against the far wall, he gave it a good yank and it pulled away from the cinder block wall to expose the door.

"Holy shit," Gabrielle muttered. "There really is a secret hiding place."

Walt pulled a key from his pocket, unlocked the padlock, and flung the door open. He turned on the overhead light and said, "Come on. It's this way." He pointed to the second door. The first door slammed behind them.

The excitement was building for Walt. It had been too long since he'd had someone in the bunker, and he was moments away from having a new woman to fulfill his needs.

Walt quickly dialed the combination on the padlock and opened the second door.

"Whoa, this is pretty cool," she said, looking into the tunnel.

"Yeah, this is my special place. Nobody else knows about it. You go first," Walt said. "I'll be right behind you." He let Gabrielle crawl head-first into the tunnel that would lead to the underground bunker. It would take a bit of maneuvering, but she was small enough that she would be able to turn around at the opposite end.

"I can't see," she hollered back to him as she entered the first few feet of the tunnel.

One of the things he'd figured out from when Joanie first entered the tunnel was to keep a flashlight handy. He didn't need it for himself since he was used to the tunnel, but for someone who wasn't familiar with the roughly eight-foot-length of tunnel, the darkness could be daunting.

He'd mounted a flashlight on the outside wall next to the tunnel. He turned it on and focused the beam above Gabrielle's head to show the path down the tunnel.

"How's that?" he asked.

"Oh, wow. That's good. I can see now."

"Keep going. I'm right behind you." Walt crawled backwards behind Gabrielle, one hand holding the flashlight in the air.

"When you get to the end, turn around and put your feet out first. You'll find a stepladder just below the opening of the tunnel," he said.

"Okay, got it. But I can't see. What is this place?"

Walt quickly backed out of the tunnel and down the small stepladder. He purposely shined the flashlight into Gabrielle's eyes, momentarily blinding her.

"What the hell, man! Now I can't see nothing but a big white dot in my eyes!"

"Oh, sorry," Walt said innocently. He turned on the floor lamp that was still in the back of the room near the tub and turned off the flashlight.

"This is your new home. You're going to be staying with me for a while." Walt offered her a smile.

"Have you lost your mind? I'm not staying here. You said there was a package you wanted me to give to someone, and you'd pay me $20. Where is it?"

"In time, my dear Little Flower. In time. But first, let me show you around."

"Little Flower?" Gabrielle repeated. "I'm not your Little Flower. You're out of your freaking mind, and I'm out of here." Gabrielle spun on her heel and turned towards the stepladder, but Walt was expecting it, grabbed her around the waist, and lifted her feet off the ground. Gabrielle tried to kick her legs and flail her arms, but he was much bigger than she was. He easily held onto her with her back pulled against his chest.

"Let me go, you asshole. Let me go!" she screamed through clenched teeth. She was sobering up quickly.

"That's it. Keep fighting, Little Flower. I like a bit of rough play."

Before long, because she was still somewhat intoxicated, she became worn out and stopped kicking. She continued to squirm in his arms, but it had little effect on him.

"Let me go," she demanded.

"Oh, but you haven't gotten the grand tour," he said. "Let me show you around."

He still had a hold of her around the middle as he walked into the bedroom. After seeing the mattress on the floor, Gabrielle clearly knew what it meant. She started kicking and fighting again.

"Don't you dare! You're crazy! Let me go!" she screamed. Walt bent his knees, and they both fell on the mattress. He had her pinned beneath him. One of his hands found her breast, and he began kneading her.

"Ow, that hurts! Get off me!" she yelled. Her struggle was less forceful now, her pleas a bit softer, her energy spent. "Why are you doing this to me?"

Walt was able to push her sweatpants down, the elastic waistband not offering any resistance at all. He was fully aroused and wasted no time in unzipping his pants and entering her. She still tried to fight him off, but it was no use, and he could tell she knew it.

When he was done, Walt stood and zipped up his pants. He tossed back his head and said, "It's been a while since I've had that kind of pleasure. I've missed it."

"You're an asshole. Just like my stepfather. He's an asshole, too." Gabrielle, with tears in her eyes, stood and pulled up her pants. "You're both assholes."

Walt looked at her without speaking for a moment. He understood what she was saying. "Your stepfather has sex with you?"

"Yes. This is not my first rodeo with abusive men. My stepfather has been raping me for a long time. He does it to me every time my mother goes to play bingo with my aunt at the community center." Her lip curled in anger as she spit the words at him.

Walt quietly held her gaze. "The toilet is in the other room if you need it. I'll bring you something to eat in a little while."

Walt turned on his heel and headed towards the tunnel. "Oh, and don't even think about trying to escape. You'll need the combination to the padlock to get out, so it won't do you any good to even try. The door is always locked, even when I'm in here, and I'm the only one who knows the combination." Walt climbed the stepladder and crawled through the tunnel.

As he locked the door behind him at the far end of the tunnel, he could hear her shouts as they echoed off the close quarters of the tunnel walls. "You're an asshole!"

Later that afternoon, Walt returned to the bunker with a small, brown lunch bag containing a hot dog, a small bag of potato chips, and a plastic bottle of water.

He found Gabrielle waiting for him at the base of the stepladder. She must have heard him coming.

"Hi. I brought you some dinner. Do you like hot dogs?" Walt lifted the bag to display it and gave her a big smile.

"Let me out of here," she demanded, with her hands on her hips. "I want to go home."

"No, I'm sorry. That won't be possible. You see, I need to keep you here for a while. But don't worry—you'll have everything you could ever want. I'll take good care of you," Walt said.

"Why did you lock the door at the end of the tunnel?" Gabrielle's eyebrows were knit together in a frown.

"Like I told you... it's so you can't get out. That sounds like you must have tried to escape. Remember, I told you the door is always locked, even when I'm here with you. That way, you can't conk me over the head and try to get away from me."

"You can't keep me here! I have a lot of friends and family that will be looking for me and when they find your ass, you'll be in so much trouble, you won't know what hit you."

She didn't sound convincing, her voice shaky. And if he was to hazard a guess, given her stepfather's proclivities, she was likely a common runaway. He laughed. "I have a lot of friends too, my Little Flower. You see, I work for the police department, and the chief is a very good friend of mine. Every once in a while, he'll come here to have sex with one of the girls that stay in my house. Girls just like you."

"You mean you've done this to other girls? You have other girls living in your house? How many?" Gabrielle tipped her head to the side to look at him out of the corner of her eyes.

"How old are you, anyway?" Walt ignored her question.

"I'm fourteen, almost fifteen."

"Really? Only fourteen? You look older than that." Walt's eyes drifted to Gabrielle's full breasts.

Gabrielle saw where his gaze landed. "Yeah, that's what my stepfather thinks, too. That's why he comes after me, just like you did."

"Let me set these down," Walt said, gesturing to the paper bag with the hot dog and chips in one hand, the water in the other. He walked into the bedroom and set the food on the overturned milk crate. Gabrielle followed him.

"What's in the bag?" she asked. She was sniffing and looked hungry.

She reached for the bag and peeked inside.

"Go ahead. Help yourself. I've already eaten," he said.

Gabrielle sat on the mattress while Walt pulled a lawn chair closer. He tried making small talk while Gabrielle ate her meal. "So, tell me about your family. Do you have any brothers or sisters?"

"Yeah, I've got one stepsister, but we don't get along. She's about seventeen. We don't have that much in common because she's always hanging out with her boyfriend and their friends."

"What do you like to do with your friends?"

"I don't know. Hang out, I guess. Drink beer, get stoned. Maybe go to the mall."

"That's cool. So, listen. I have a few rules here that I need to explain." Walt rubbed his palms on his pant legs.

"What are you talking about?" Gabrielle gulped down the last bite of hot dog. "What rules?"

Walt explained he would be bringing her meals, along with magazines and whatever else she might want. "Your job is to have sex with me whenever I want, and I'll make sure you're happy here."

"You're out of your freaking mind. I'm not some whore you can keep in this place forever." She crinkled the brown paper bag into a ball and threw it at Walt, hitting him in the chest.

Walt stood up, making sure he towered over her as she sat on the mattress. "You will do as you are told. Remember, I have a lot of powerful friends. The chief of police, political people, and even someone in the FBI." With that, Walt pushed her down onto the mattress and raped her again.

CHAPTER SEVEN

Unbeknownst to Gabrielle, she was living the same type of life in the bunker as her predecessor. He would give her meals sporadically. She was forced to write an S, B or T on a calendar that Walt provided, and he raped her every single day. However, the one big difference between them was that Joanie had become more withdrawn and depressed as time went on, always in fear for her family after Walt's constant threats to harm them.

Gabrielle, however, heard the same threats Joanie had heard, but she wasn't as close to her family as Joanie, so the threats didn't carry as much weight.

Gabrielle was more of a fighter and had spent time on the streets, which made her a tougher, more combative hostage. Nonetheless, she was still only fourteen years old, and the tough persona on the outside would crumble when she was alone, especially during the long and lonely nights.

One of her constant fears was becoming pregnant with Walt's child. She finally expressed her concern to Walt but tried to use it to her advantage. "You need to let me go," she said, "before I get pregnant. It's not like I'm on birth control or anything."

"Weren't you on the pill when your stepfather was having sex with you?" Walt asked.

"No, I wasn't on the pill. He used a condom, but you're not using one and I don't want to get pregnant," she said.

"You don't have to worry. I had a vasectomy years ago. Now that you know you're not going to get knocked up, come here and give me a little loving," he said with a lascivious smile.

Not long after she'd been kidnapped, Gabrielle spotted what looked to be a small paint can tucked in the corner behind the tub. She eagerly grabbed the can and the stiff, paint-encrusted brush that had been resting on top of the can. She shook the can and could hear sloshing inside, and the drips on the label told her the paint was red, like the color of old bricks. Gabrielle looked around the bunker, trying to decide what to do with the newfound paint. It didn't feel like there was enough paint to cover a wall, but maybe she could paint a picture somewhere. Then again, what kind of picture could she paint with just one color? She'd have to think about it. It was a precious find to someone whose days ran one into the other with no diversion and she didn't want to waste the paint.

Gabrielle quickly discovered there was no way to open the can because the lid was stuck tight from the dried paint collected around its edges. It was as if the lid was glued to the can with cement.

Roaming throughout the bunker, she couldn't find anything strong enough to break through the dried paint and pry the lid off. She put the can back where she'd found it, just on the odd chance Walt would notice it had been moved and would be angry with her, or worse, take it away. She would have to wait to decorate her walls until such time as she could find a screwdriver or something similar to open the can.

Two days later, Walt brought her dinner—cold, canned stew, a slice of unbuttered bread—and a metal spoon! Her eyes opened wide when she noticed the spoon. He usually made it a practice to bring plastic utensils, just in case, he had said, she got any funny ideas to stab him with a knife or fork. The plastic utensils would break before they could injure him, he rationalized. Today, he must have figured a metal spoon was not a dangerous weapon.

He stayed for a few minutes to chat with her. She purposely ate slowly, making the meal last longer than it normally did. He left before she finished eating, leaving the dinner plate and the precious spoon behind.

Gabrielle put the stew aside and ran to the entrance of the tunnel to listen. Barely breathing, she heard the thump as the door at the far end closed. As soon as the coast was clear, she grabbed the paint can and used the handle of the spoon to pry off the lid. It was a struggle, but eventually the dried paint gave way, and the lid popped off. The spoon was bent, now resembling a horseshoe more than a spoon, but she would do her best to straighten it later.

With a smile, Gabrielle walked into the bedroom with the can in one hand, the brush in the other. She stood on the mattress and dipped the brush in the paint. In big, bold, capital letters, she wrote "GABRIELLE WUZ HERE 2015."

She stood back and surveyed her handiwork. She was on a roll and felt energized, maybe even a bit rebellious. Gabrielle looked around the room for another open spot and decided to paint a peace sign on the wall near the doorway. She then went into the bath area and drew another peace sign in there. On another wall, she wrote, "Ready to ruckus so bring on the pain" and "wall of thugs."

As she looked at her artwork, sadness overwhelmed her. Would she ever get out? How many other girls had been held in the dungeon as a victim of Walt's? He said there were girls in his house that his friends visited for sex. Were they also being held against their will? How many were there?

Gabrielle climbed the stepladder to the opening to the tunnel. Over the opening, she carefully and meticulously painted the words, "Peace to all who enter here." As she looked at the words, teardrops of wet paint left a red path down the wall. A tear of her own fell down her cheek. She felt hopeless. According to the calendar he'd given her to mark S, B and T, she had been in this hellhole for two months. It seemed like a lifetime.

The next day, Gabrielle was sitting in the lawn chair near the tub as Walt climbed down the ladder into the dungeon. She was apprehensive as he faced the room and discovered the graffiti she'd painted on the walls. She held her breath. Would he be mad? Would he punish her? Hit her?

Walt stood for a moment, looking at the walls, then walked into the mattress room without saying a word. He came back to stand in front of Gabrielle. He wore a blank expression on his face, one that Gabrielle couldn't read. She barely breathed as she waited to see what his reaction would be.

"Where did you get the paint?" he asked.

"It was behind the tub." Gabrielle pointed to the corner of the room where the paint can was hidden.

"Do you want more?"

Gabrielle's eyes opened wide in surprise. "Do I want more paint?" she asked.

"Yes, do you want more paint?"

"Sure," Gabrielle said excitedly. She had thought for sure she'd be in trouble, so she was very relieved he wasn't upset with her.

It would be a few weeks before he remembered to bring her more paint, and even then, it was only two small tubes of artist's paint. Although it was a trivial item to Walt, Gabrielle saw it as a momentary break from the constant boredom she faced on a daily, if not hourly basis, and she welcomed it.

Time passed in agonizing fashion, Gabrielle having been Walt's captive for four months. The time in the dungeon had been difficult, to say the least. The rapes and loneliness had broken her spirit. She had turned fifteen but didn't even bother to tell Walt about her birthday. As a hostage, she didn't feel anything was worth celebrating.

One afternoon, Walt entered the dungeon to find Gabrielle sitting in the lawn chair listening to the portable radio, the volume high enough to make conversation difficult. She didn't even look up anymore when he stepped down from the tunnel into the bunker. A non-existent hangnail suddenly caught her attention.

"Hey, Little Flower. What kind of music is that?" he asked, as he reached over and turned it down a bit.

"Really? What do you mean 'what kind of music'? It's hip hop." She looked at him as if he had the intelligence of a houseplant.

"Ah. Well, I listen mostly to country music," he said. "Can you dance to that hip hop stuff?"

"Yeah, I guess so. Why?"

"Will you show me?"

"Are you serious?" She looked at him skeptically. "You want to learn how to dance to hip hop music?"

"Sure. I'd like to learn. Will you teach me?"

Gabrielle looked at him for a long moment before answering. "I guess so." With a sigh, she got out of the chair and pushed it closer to the wall, giving them more room for the dance lesson.

The song playing on the radio was fuzzy from static, but it was good enough for Gabrielle to dance to. Walt stood opposite her and imitated her movements as best he could. Where she was fluid with her style, he was choppy, but neither one seemed to care, although for different reasons.

If she had been with her friends, Gabrielle would have enjoyed the moment, but with Walt, she just went through the motions.

When the song ended, Walt clapped his hands, a wide smile lighting up his face. "That was fun. I really enjoyed that. Thank you, Little Flower, for showing me how to dance to hip hop music."

"Why do you call me that?"

"What? Little Flower?"

"Yes. Why do you call me that? What does it mean?"

"Well, I love to garden, and I have a lot of flower beds around the outside of the house, especially roses. My wife loved them also. I think they're beautiful, and they're very special to me. That's why I call you my Little Flower. You're very special to me, too. Someday I might even call you my Little Rose, but you have to be a very good girl and earn that title."

Gabrielle turned away without saying a word. She turned off the radio and sat in the lawn chair, going back to the hang nail that didn't exist. Walt moved towards her, intent on continuing to have what he clearly perceived to be more fun.

CHAPTER EIGHT

Once a fourteen-year-old, street-wise kid who skipped school, smoked weed, and drank alcohol for fun, Gabrielle became a shell of her former self. After eight months in the dungeon, she'd lost weight and looked almost skeletal. Her eyes, sunken in with dark circles below, had lost their spark. She rarely talked and spent most of her time sleeping. When Walt brought her food, she only picked at it, rarely finishing the meal.

Walt had no compassion for his captives, but even he began to notice something was definitely wrong. Gabrielle's condition was deteriorating. She no longer resisted when he came to her for sex. She simply laid on the mattress, letting him do whatever he wanted. Her spirit was truly broken.

Walt decided the time had come to let Gabrielle go before she needed a doctor, or worse, something happened to her. He would have to act quickly. Besides, it was no fun for him to have sex with someone who just laid there.

Early one morning, a few days after he'd made the decision to release her, Walt woke Gabrielle. "C'mon, Little Rose. Wake up. You're going for a ride."

Gabrielle slowly opened her eyes. "What did you say?" Her voice was scratchy.

"I need you to get up. I'm taking you for a ride." Walt pulled on her arm and tried to lift her into an upright position. She was dead weight and didn't try to stand up on her own.

"Are you going to kill me?" Gabrielle asked, her voice soft, more from listlessness than fright.

"Of course not. I just need to run an errand, and I want you to come with me. Stand up."

As Gabrielle stood, Walt handed her a bag. "Put them on," he pointed to the bag. She peeked inside and saw her own clothes; the ones she'd been wearing on the day he kidnapped her. She hadn't seen them since that day, having only worn odd thrift-store castoffs in the meantime.

As she lifted her clothes from the bag, something fell to the floor. She looked down and saw the shiny plastic of her school ID laying on the cold concrete floor, her own face staring back at her. Her home address was listed on the back of the card.

The ID should have been in the back pocket of her sweats, but if it was loose, that could mean Walt had gone through her pockets and found it. He might know where she lived, but would that matter if he was keeping her locked up in the dungeon forever?

Once she had dressed, Walt spun her around to face away from him. He pulled a folded bandana from his pocket and wrapped it around her head, covering her eyes.

"Why are you blindfolding me? I don't like that. Take it off!" She reached up to remove the cloth from her eyes, but Walt was quicker. He grabbed her wrists and yanked her hands away before she pulled off the bandana.

"No, you need to leave it on. I don't want you to see where we're going."

"How am I supposed to get through the tunnel and all the shit you've got in the basement if I can't see?"

"Hmm," Walt mumbled. "You're right. Okay, I'll take it off for now, but it goes back on as soon as we're out of the tunnel."

With the bandana off her head, Gabrielle crawled to the end of the tunnel where, true to his word, Walt repositioned the bandana over her eyes. He weaved a zig-zag path through the maze of shelves in the basement with one hand on her elbow. He led her outdoors—she knew that because she could feel the cool morning air on her arms—and assisted her into the car.

She heard the car engine roar to life, and her stomach twisted into a knot as thoughts ran through her mind. *Why the blindfold? What kind of errand does he want to run? Can I trust him not to kill me? But so what if he killed me? Life isn't worth living if I have to spend the rest of my life in a damp, dark, underground room with no one but Walt to talk to and doing nothing but having sex with him.* Gabrielle settled into the car seat, ready to accept whatever happened to her.

"Listen to me," said Walt. "You need to remember that I have a lot of powerful friends, including the police chief. He's a good buddy of mine. I know a lot of people—important people—and you need to remember that, okay?"

"Yeah, sure. Whatever," Gabrielle said.

After a while, Gabrielle felt the car slow to a stop and heard the gear shift slide into the park position. With no warning, Walt ripped the bandana from her head, taking a few strands of hair with it. Gabrielle blinked as her eyes adjusted to the blinding sunshine, a sight she hadn't seen in over eight months. Through the tears brought on by the brightness, she looked out the side window, and her family's home came into focus.

She never even looked back at Walt. Her hand found the door handle, her eyes stayed focused on the house. She bolted for the front door, leaving the car door open behind her.

"Remember what I said!" she heard Walt yell from behind her as she sprinted up the sidewalk. She thought she'd never see her family again, and now, for once in her life, she was happy to see them.

Gabrielle bounded up the front steps and ran through the front door so fast, the door slammed against the inside wall, leaving a dent from the doorknob.

"Mom? Tina! Jay! Mom, where are you? I'm home!" Gabrielle yelled as she ran from room to room, looking for her family.

When they heard the thunderous noise, the family came running from different directions. They quickly gathered around her, welcoming her home. Her mother cried and smothered her in hugs and kisses, while her stepfather, Jay, welcomed her home with a firm pat on the back. Even her stepsister, Tina, gave her a hug.

Gabrielle spent the rest of the morning sharing her story of the previous eight months with her family. She cried as she disclosed the details, while the family listened with only a few interruptions. By the end of her tale, Gabrielle had turned angry. The spark, the fight, and the spirit had come back to her.

"He warned me not to go to the cops, but I'm going to. He said there was another girl he'd held captive before me. I don't know if she reported him, but I doubt it. If she had reported him, he would have been in jail."

"Are you sure you want to do that? He said he knows the police chief, and we don't want any trouble," asked Jay, her stepfather.

"I don't give a shit if he knows the President of the United States." Gabrielle glared at her stepfather. "The man raped me every single day for eight months! He needs to be stopped before he does it to someone else!"

Gabrielle gave Jay a disgusted look. She turned to her mother and said, "I'm going to take a shower. When I'm done, I'm going to the police station."

Gabrielle stood under the warm spray of the shower and scrubbed her skin until it was red and shiny. She needed to scrub hard to clean off the filth from Walter. After a length of time, the water turned ice cold, too cold to stay under the stream of water any longer.

As she got dressed, she realized her clothes were now very loose on her and didn't fit as they had before. She'd lost more weight than she'd realized. Luckily, she had a pair of sweatpants with a drawstring and could pull it tight. It didn't matter that the matching sweatshirt was also too large. She preferred a larger size anyway, which gave her more room.

Gabrielle went downstairs after tying her hair, still damp from the shower, into a ponytail. She found her mother and stepfather whispering together at the kitchen table, but they stopped talking when she entered the room.

She looked at them cautiously. "What's going on?"

"Nothing, dear," said her mother.

"Nothing at all," said her stepfather.

"Yeah, right," Gabrielle said. "Whatever." Apparently, some things would never change. "Look, I'm going to the police department now. I should be back in a little while." She turned on her heel and headed towards the front door.

"Gabrielle, wait," her mother said, as she got up from the table.

Gabrielle stopped but didn't turn around. "What?"

"Do you want me to take you?" her mother asked softly.

Gabrielle turned towards her mother and was silent for a moment. She looked in her mother's eyes and saw concern. "Yeah, okay. Sure."

Her mother smiled and grabbed her purse from the small table near the door.

The ride in her mother's van was quiet, with neither one saying a word for the few minutes it took to drive to the police department. As her mother parked in the lot, she reached over and put her hand on Gabrielle's knee. Gabrielle flinched at the sudden touch, an uncontrollable reaction after living with a sexual predator for so long.

"I know I haven't always been the best mother, but I want you to know I was really worried about you when you were gone. I just want to say I'm here for you, baby, and I love you."

Gabrielle looked at her mother and saw her eyes glistening with unshed tears. "I love you too, Mom." She gave her mother's hand a squeeze. "Let's do this. I want to catch this asshole."

CHAPTER NINE

Gabrielle and her mother had to wait only a few minutes before an officer joined them in the conference room.

"Hi, I'm Officer Steve MacIntosh." He held out his hand to Gabrielle and her mother.

"Hi, I'm Gabrielle Reyes, and this is my mother, Juanita Dexter."

He pulled out a chair and sat down. "What can I do for you?" the officer asked, looking between mother and daughter.

"I was kidnapped and held for eight months in some kind of underground dungeon and raped every single day by an old man named Walt. He's an asshole and you need to arrest his ass."

Officer MacIntosh blinked for a few seconds, taking a moment to absorb what Gabrielle had said.

He wasn't sure he heard her correctly. "Let's start at the beginning, so I understand this. When were you kidnapped?" he asked.

"I don't remember the exact date, but I know it was eight months ago because he made me keep a calendar. He made me use a red crayon, and I had to write on the calendar whenever he let me take a bath,"—Gabrielle held up her hand and raised her index finger—"and whenever he let me brush my teeth,"—she raised her middle finger—"and every time we had sex,"—she raised her ring finger—"which was at least once a day, every day."

Gabrielle then began to tell her story for the second time that day. Ofc. MacIntosh had a small notebook he'd pulled from his pocket and began writing copious notes. He would occasionally interrupt, but only when he needed clarification on some details.

Ofc. MacIntosh asked Gabrielle if she knew her captor's full name, but all she knew was that he had asked her to call him Walt. She described him as being an older man, at least fifty years old, average height and weight, balding but with a ring of white hair around the lower half of his head, and a closely cropped white beard and mustache. He wore large, old-fashioned eyeglasses, and usually wore khaki pants with old, threadbare polo shirts when the weather was warm or worn, flannel shirts when it was colder.

Mac asked Gabrielle when she had gotten away and was surprised to learn she'd been released just a few hours before. "I don't know why he released me now after eight months of living in hell. He just came into the dungeon this morning, woke me up, and said he wanted to take me for a ride. I thought he was going to kill me, but he said he had to run an errand and wanted me to go with him. He put a bandana over my eyes before he walked me to the car so I couldn't see his house or what street he lived on.

"Next thing I know, he stopped the car and ripped off the bandana. He'd stopped in front of my parent's house, so I got out of the car and ran like hell into the house. I never even looked back. The strange thing is, I don't know how he knew where I lived. I think he found out because I had my school ID with me when he kidnapped me, and the address was on the back."

Ofc. MacIntosh asked if she knew where Walt lived, but she only knew she'd been living in an underground concrete room. She had no idea where it was located, but she sheepishly admitted to being drunk when he'd kidnapped her. She thought she must have fallen asleep in the car on the way to the dungeon because she couldn't remember how she got there. Gabrielle gave a sideways glance to her mother as she said this. Her mom had looked down at her hands in her lap, obviously not happy with her daughter's admission to being drunk. Gabrielle admitted to Mac her underage drinking had always been a bone of contention between mother and daughter.

"Did he say why he was taking you home? Why now? Why not before?" Mac asked.

"I have no idea why he was kicking me free. He never said a word about it, and I didn't even know that's where we were going until he parked the car in front of my house. He had only told me we were going to be running some kind of errand; He never said he was taking me home.

"But he must have been planning to release me for a while, though, because he told me a bunch of times... actually, the whole time I was there... not to go to the police, or else. He must have figured I would get out someday."

"What did he say would happen if you went to the police?" Mac asked.

Gabrielle explained how Walt claimed to be "good friends with men in high places," saying he knew the chief of police, among others. He told her if she reported him to the police, he would find out from his friend the chief, and either he or one of his buddies would come after her and her family.

"Can you tell me what the dungeon looked like?" Mac asked.

Gabrielle went on to describe the basement full of bottles and cans, but because of her alcohol-addled brain at the time she was kidnapped, her memory wasn't clear on the details. And as she was leaving, she was too scared to pay attention to the multitude of shelves and bottles. Her mind was sorting through the different scenarios that Walt might do to her. She was better able to describe the underground bunker, the bathtub, the toilet, and the room with the mattress. She told him about painting the peace signs and things like "GABRIELLE WUZ HERE 2015" on the walls.

"He liked to call me his 'Little Flower' and 'Little Rose' because he considered me to be as precious as his favorite flower." She spit the words out with disgust. "He described quite often his many rose gardens on his property."

"Hmm," Mac said. "A house with multiple rose gardens could be a possible clue when identifying this Walt guy." He underlined the notation regarding the rose gardens in his notebook.

"If you don't mind," Mac said, "I'd like to take you to the hospital to see if we could collect his DNA from you or from your clothes. Would you be willing to do that?"

Gabrielle thought for a moment before saying, "I would, but I already took a shower after I got home this morning. Does that matter?"

"It might. The DNA is probably gone, but we could use your clothes, especially your underwear. Do you still have any clothes from when you were in the bunker?"

"No, I don't have any of the clothes I wore when I was there. It's embarrassing, but he never gave me any underwear except when I had my period. He always supplied me with sweatpants and sweatshirts, though, and every couple of weeks, he'd give me freshly laundered sweats, but he must still have them.

"The thing that's weird is he gave me back my own clothes this morning, the ones I had on when he kidnapped me. I just thought it was because the sweats he gave me were old and faded, and he wanted me to look nicer since we were supposedly going out in public.

"The other thing that's really weird is that he hadn't had sex with me for the last four days. I don't know why, but I sure as hell wasn't going to ask."

Mac underlined that notation in his notebook as well. Did this guy stop having sex with Gabrielle, knowing he was going to release her, so there would be no DNA to track?

It took over an hour to relay all the information Gabrielle had to offer to Ofc. MacIntosh. By the time they were done, Gabrielle admitted to Mac and her mother she felt energized, as if a weight had been lifted from her shoulders, but at the same time, she felt exhausted. All she wanted to do was go home, she said, crawl into her own bed, and sleep.

Gabrielle's mother, Juanita, had sat quietly throughout the entire conversation, occasionally wincing as her daughter described her ordeal in detail. It was difficult for a mom to hear about the abuse her daughter had gone through.

Secretly vowing to show more love to her daughter, Juanita would begin by addressing Gabrielle's concerns about the attention her husband, Jay—Gabrielle's stepfather—had been giving Gabrielle before the kidnapping. She had always felt that something was wrong between them. It seemed as if Gabrielle avoided him like the plague, and yet he wanted to spend as much time with her as possible.

She promised herself she would find out what caused her stomach to clench whenever she saw him looking at Gabrielle in that strange way. If her suspicions proved to be true, she would kick him to the curb in a heartbeat.

CHAPTER TEN

Ofc. MacIntosh couldn't believe what he had heard. A sexual predator had kidnapped a young teenager and raped her daily for months. But how was he supposed to find this guy? There was virtually nothing to go on.

Normally, his assignment was to work on the road as a patrol officer, but this type of case would require him to work in the office, doing research on the computer. Ofc. MacIntosh decided he would run it past his supervisor, to see if he could take the time from the road to work on the investigation.

"Hey, Mac. What's up?" Sergeant Greene removed his glasses as he looked up when Ofc. MacIntosh entered the office.

"I just took a statement from a young girl that was kidnapped eight months ago and was held as a sex slave in an underground bunker. She described her kidnapper, but it's pretty vague. Just his first name and physical description. That's it."

"Hmm… that's not much to go on. She didn't have an address for this guy?" Greene asked.

"No. Nothing. The only thing I know is that he must be local, and that's because, when he released her, he drove her to her home, but the ride only took a short while. He had her blindfolded so she couldn't see the route they traveled.

"I'm going to check the local sex offender registry for anyone with the first name of Walt or Walter. I'm also going to see if I can find someone with an MO of keeping his captives in a bunker or a dungeon."

"Well," said Greene, "it's a start. If you need extra help, we'll talk to the Criminal Investigation Division and see if they have any ideas. For now, I'll pull you from the road. Just stay on the case and see what you can come up with but keep me posted. This guy definitely needs to be caught." The sergeant put his glasses on and returned to the report he was reading.

Mac worked for hours, trying to find something that would lead him to Walt, but he drew a blank. He wasn't even sure that was the guy's real name. And the sex offender registry had no one local who kept his victims imprisoned in a bunker. He could try the national sex offender registry for anyone outside the Gaithersburg area, but that wouldn't do much good if the man was clearly living in the area.

He even ran a search of motor vehicle records of men in the area named Walt or Walter, but several hundred were listed. Without a warrant for each one, he couldn't go knocking on their doors to see if they had a bunker.

After exhausting all avenues that he could think of, Mac walked into the Criminal Investigation Division, commonly referred to as CID.

"I was hoping you guys could help me on a case," Mac said.

"Sure," said Investigator Tony Donatella. "What do you have?"

Mac was glad Tony was available to help. The investigator had worked for the police department for over twenty-five years, with over fifteen of them in CID. He had talked of retiring next year but so far, hadn't given a firm date. It was his position that Mac hoped to fill.

Mac relayed Gabrielle's story, then filled Tony in on the information—or rather, the lack of information—he had gathered from his internet searches.

"It sounds like you covered all the bases, Mac. I don't know what more you can do. It would be helpful if we had more details from her testimony, but even then, we still might not have enough to find this guy."

"Yeah, that's just it. I've got nothing to go by. I can't even break it down to a certain area because she wasn't sure how long it took to drive her home, whether it was fifteen minutes or an hour. She was afraid he was going to kill her, so she wasn't paying attention to how much time she spent in the car."

"Unfortunately, until such time as the victim remembers something else that would help, or God forbid, we have another victim come forward, we'll have to hope something pops up," said Tony, shaking his head.

Discouraged but still determined, Mac promised himself he'd keep the case in the forefront of his mind until he could find this "Walt" character.

CHAPTER ELEVEN

Walt was getting antsy. He hadn't had a woman confined to the bunker since he'd released Gabrielle months before, and he was getting desperate for some female companionship.

Walt's son, Gregory, had moved back home for a while after he and his wife split up. Walt knew better than to have a woman in the bunker while his son was in the house. Gregory didn't know about the bunker, the women that had been living in there, or Walt's obsession with sex. It would not be wise to let Gregory in on his secrets. Walt believed in the adage, "What he doesn't know won't keep him up nights wondering."

Thankfully, Gregory had now moved out, so Walt was free to bring another female into his lair. He would have to go out on the prowl to see if he could find someone to bring to his bunker, and soon.

Walt drove slowly through the residential neighborhoods, his car windows down in the warm August air. He spotted a fair amount of women who were out and about enjoying after-dinner walks.

Unfortunately, they were with other people, or he didn't find them attractive.

After driving around for an hour, he finally saw a woman with long black hair that caught his eye. She was sitting on a bench at a bus stop, reading a book. With her head down, he couldn't see her face, but she appeared to be alone. That was good enough.

Walt drove past the woman and pulled a U-turn so he could park on the same side of the street. He parked next to the curb about twenty feet away from the woman and watched her for several minutes. No one else joined her at the bus stop, and as he looked around, he could see the street was fairly deserted. What few people were on the street were a ways away. It was as if God had given Walt a gift.

He inched the car closer to the woman and jumped out, leaving the car running. She never even looked up as Walt quickly approached her from behind.

As soon as she felt the strong arms wrap around her torso from underneath her armpits, the woman began screaming, but it was a futile effort. No one was around to hear her. Still, he cupped his hand over her mouth to muffle the screams. Her book fell to the ground as he forcefully pulled her from the bus stop. He dragged her, kicking and screaming, to the car and pushed her into the back seat. She laid on the seat, too afraid to sit up. She covered her face with her hands and wept.

To Walt, the moment was exhilarating. He had gone without a woman to satisfy his sexual urges long enough. He didn't want to wait any longer. A few blocks away was an abandoned building that had at one time, been a warehouse. He knew this because he was the owner of the building. He would take her there.

The woman was crying in the back seat and speaking some kind of Asian language. It was gibberish to Walt, but it didn't matter. It wasn't her conversation he was interested in.

He drove around the six-foot wire fence that surrounded the red brick warehouse to make sure no one else was there. He had it listed with a real estate agent who might show the property at any given time, but with no other cars in the parking lot, it appeared to be empty. Perfect!

Walt stopped in front of the wire gate, inserted a key in the lock, and pushed the gate open. After he drove into the parking lot, he closed the gate behind him. If she got away from him and ran, she wouldn't get far.

He drove to a side door and stepped onto the pavement at the same time he put the car in park. The car lurched to a sudden stop. He opened the back door, grabbed his victim, and pulled her out of the car by her legs. Taking hold of her by the arm, he forced her to walk towards the building.

Walt winced as the woman let out a blood-curdling scream. He quickly cupped his hand over her mouth to silence her and wrapped his other hand tightly around her waist. Lifting her off the ground, he carried her towards the building.

As he approached the door, he removed a set of keys from his pants pocket but left his other hand around her waist. She twisted and turned, trying to break free of his hold. When that didn't work, she leaned over and bit his arm. In a knee-jerk reaction, he slapped her—hard—on the side of her head.

Stunned by the sudden, intense pain, the woman stopped fighting him. She put her hand to her ear as the tears ran down her cheeks.

Within seconds, he had her pinned on the cold cement floor, ripped off her clothes, and raped her. She had tried everything in her power to resist, but the pain was too great. She had no energy left to fight off the much bigger man.

As he knelt over her, Walt felt better now that he'd released some of that pent-up energy. He looked at his victim. She held her hands over her eyes and was quietly crying. He pulled both of her hands away so he might get a better look at her.

She was Asian, rather petite, both in height and size. He thought she was about fifty years old, but with red, puffy eyes held tightly closed, it was hard to tell.

He realized, in his urgency, he'd ripped her lightweight cotton pants almost in half, and the silk blouse was torn and missing most of the buttons. There's no way she'd be able to wear them. The shirt might cover some of her front, but the pants would fall off as soon as he put them on her. And yet he couldn't take her back to his house with no clothes. If anyone saw her like that, Walt would get in trouble for sure, especially if he got stopped by a cop.

He looked around the warehouse and saw a stack of old, wavy cardboard in a corner. It wasn't much better than having her completely naked, but he could make it work. He grabbed two pieces of the cardboard, each about three feet long, and wiped off the dust and cobwebs. Walt used the arms of her torn shirt to tie the cardboard onto her, with one piece covering her front, the other covering her back.

Walt led her out of the building. She had to walk to the car with baby steps because the cardboard ran past her knees. She clumsily maneuvered herself into the back seat with no choice but to lie down. Sitting was not an option because of the stiffness of the cardboard.

Walt drove around for nearly an hour until the sun began to set. Although his house was fairly hidden from the neighbors, thanks to the tall arborvitae, he would take advantage of the additional cover from the darkening sky while he brought his captive into the house. It wasn't until he had her in the basement that he realized there was no way she'd be able to manage the tunnel or the ladder while she was draped in the stiff cardboard. He removed the cardboard as she cried silent tears.

He pointed to the opening to the tunnel and said rather loudly, "You need to go through there. Crawl on your hands and knees. Go on, go!"

She crawled through the tunnel and into the bunker, naked, with Walt following directly behind.

Seeing her naked aroused Walt again. He had gone too long without sexual gratification, so, for the second time that evening, once they found their way into the bunker, he wanted sex from his victim.

She tried fighting off his advances, but it was no use. Once she began resisting, he put his hands around her neck and choked her into submission. When he finally released his hold on her, she began coughing, trying to catch her breath.

Her natural reaction was to roll onto her side, but Walt repeatedly tried to force her onto her back. Frustrated at not being able to enter her, he hauled off and slapped her. He meant to connect with her cheek, but when she kept trying to shift to her side, he ended up slapping her ear. It was the same side of her head that he'd connected with only a few hours before.

The woman was stunned, the pain immediate and fierce. She began crying hysterically, her sobs causing her to cough even more. Walt pinned her down by the shoulders and finished what he started out to do.

When Walt was done, the woman could finally shift onto her side, her hand cupping her ear. A trickle of blood ran down her cheek. Little did they know, the damage Walt had inflicted on her eardrum would end up being a permanent reminder of the abuse she suffered at his hand.

Walt left her laying in a heap on the floor and went back to his house, a satisfied smile on his lips.

An hour later, Walt went back into the bunker to talk to his captive. She was in the same spot on the floor as she was when he'd left. However, when she looked up and saw him climbing down the ladder, she quickly crab walked, still naked, towards the wall behind her.

"No! No! No!" she yelled at him.

He stood in front of her. "What's your name?" Walt asked. She responded with a flurry of jumbled words in a language he did not understand. She put both hands up in front of her, as if she was blocking him from approaching.

"Do you speak English?" he asked.

"No, no Engrish," she said.

"Not even a little English?"

"No Engrish," she said again.

Hmm. That could be a problem, he thought.

In one hand, Walt held a plate of food. In the other, he held a bag. "I brought you some clothes." He tossed the bag to the floor in front of her. "My wife passed away several years ago, but I never found the time or the energy to throw away her clothes. There's a pair of sweatpants and a sweatshirt in the bag. They're probably too big, but it's better than nothing.

"I also brought you some dinner." Walt made a motion with one hand to simulate putting food to his mouth. He held out the plate he'd been holding. "Do you like chicken?"

She looked at the plate of chicken nuggets and French fries, then looked back at Walt. He couldn't read her expression, but if anything, she looked as if she had no idea what kind of food it was that sat on the plate. Walt picked up a French fry and ate it. He said, "Mmm. It's good," as he rubbed his belly.

She only shook her head at the food and continued to talk in a strange language. Walt left the plate on the overturned milk crate and left.

The next morning, Walt returned to the bunker. He found the woman curled up in a ball on the mattress, sound asleep, but wearing the clothes he'd brought to her the night before. He stood next to her for a few moments, looking at her. Finally, he reached down and shook her shoulder. She jumped as she woke, suddenly aware he was there.

"Hey, it's okay. Don't get scared." Walt held his hands up, palms outward, in a sign of surrender. She looked at him, her eyes wide. "I really wish you knew English," he said. "This is going to be difficult trying to talk to you."

Walt shook his head, and with a frustrated sigh, he left through the tunnel.

Later that day, Walt was in the basement adding more beer bottles to his collection when he heard singing coming from the bunker. It was a song he'd heard many times before, back in the day when he and his wife went to church. If he remembered correctly, the song was called *How Great Thou Art.*

He made his way slowly through the tunnel, wanting to get closer but not wanting to alert her he was coming. He didn't want her to stop singing. She had a wonderful singing voice.

The song ended, and Walt made his way down the stepladder and into the bunker.

"That was really good! You're a great singer!" It was then that he realized she had sung in English. Perfect English, as a matter of fact. "Hey, wait a minute. How come you sang that in English? You *do* speak English, don't you?"

His captive raised her chin and said again, "No Engrish."

"Knock it off. I don't believe you. So, tell me, what's your name?"

After a few moments, she lowered her eyes to stare at the floor. "Yes, I do speak English."

"Why did you lie to me?" asked Walt.

"I'm afraid of you."

"You don't have to be afraid of me. I'm not going to hurt you," he said.

"How can I not be afraid of you? And you've already hurt me terribly. You've raped me and slapped me. My ear was bleeding and still hurts like hell. What do you mean, you will not hurt me? You already did!" She raised her voice, almost to a yell. At the sound of her own raised voice, she cringed. Her hand went protectively to her ear.

"Yeah, well, I'm sorry I hit you. I didn't mean to hurt your ear."

"You need to let me go. My family will be looking for me, and you're going to be in big trouble when they hear what you've done to me."

"No, I won't let you go, and I won't be in any kind of trouble. You see, I'm good friends with a lot of powerful men in powerful positions, including the chief of police and a couple of FBI men. And if you don't behave yourself, they're apt to stop in, and they'll want to, uh, spend time with you like I do. There are other girls that live in the house, and they've been there for a long time. Their job is to satisfy my friends. If you try to escape, I'll move you into the house with the girls. Then it won't be just me you'll have sex with, it will be a lot of different men."

"You can't be serious." Her eyes grew wide, her voice almost a whisper.

"I'm dead serious. For now, you're going to stay here and have sex with me whenever I want it, and in return, I'll make sure you're taken care of. I'll bring you food and magazines, you've got a radio, and there's a bathtub and toilet in the other room. But you're going to stay here until I say you can leave."

Her knees gave way at the realization of his words, and she collapsed onto the bed.

That proved to be a mistake.

Walt took advantage of her position on the mattress and raped her yet again. When he was done, he asked her for her name.

In tears, she told him her name was Yen Nguyen.

"Will you sing me a song, Yen? You sing really well."

"I don't feel like singing," she said.

"Where did you learn to sing like that?" he asked.

"I sing in the church choir." She hung her head and said, "You have brought me shame because of what you've done to me. I can't imagine what the priest would think of me if he knew."

Walt looked at his watch and said, "I didn't realize it was that late. I need to get going, but I'll be back later with some food. Oh, and don't even think about trying to escape. I lock the doors at all times, even when I'm here with you. I'm the only one who knows the combination to the lock, so it won't do you any good to try to get out." With that, Walt climbed up the stepladder and disappeared into the tunnel.

He stopped a few feet into the tunnel to listen. He could hear her collapse onto the mattress and cry herself to sleep.

CHAPTER TWELVE

In time, Yen learned that the best way to avoid any further slaps from Walt was to sing to him or make him laugh. But if, for some reason, his temper reared its ugly head, she risked being on the receiving end of his slaps.

After one instance when he'd slapped her for refusing to satisfy him the way he'd wanted, he blamed her for his fits of anger. It was her fault he put his hands on her, he'd said. It was her fault because she wasn't listening to his demands and wasn't performing as he expected her to.

He also confessed that he'd never hit any of the other girls; she was the first one he'd ever struck. If she did what she was supposed to do, he wouldn't have to hit her. After all, he told her, she should be thankful since he gave her everything she could possibly need, and as a woman, it was her duty to satisfy him.

Yen knew enough to know this was an attempt to control her, but she also realized the importance of his statements. It meant that, possibly, his temper was getting worse with time, but more importantly, there may have been other captives in the bunker. He could be referring to the women that lived in the house—he'd said something about them once before when he'd first abducted her. However, if he had other captives who had been held in the bunker, that would explain the messages painted on the walls. Until then, she had thought the messages must have been written by his kids years ago. She'd never asked him, just assumed he had kids, and they played there.

She learned early on that he hated crying, so she kept her tears to herself. She never cried when he was around, although it was hard not to cry when he was abusing her.

To appease him, she listened to the radio and learned the country songs that Walt preferred. She sang to him as often as she could. After all, "Music hath charms to soothe the savage breast." That fit Walt to a tee.

The singing came easily to Yen, so she used her talent as often as she could as a means to keep Walt in a good mood. She also learned from him that he enjoyed a good chuckle, but making Walt laugh was another story. Given her circumstances, she struggled to talk to him with humor. Her son, however, was a jokester, so regaling Walt with his antics seemed to help. The irony was that the stories about her son made Walt laugh, but they made Yen cry. Still, she held her tears until Walt left the bunker. She had always loved and appreciated her son and his sense of humor, now more than ever.

After Walt had held Yen captive in the dungeon for about a month, Walt asked her to clean his house.

"I have a lot of stuff in the house, my Little Flower, and it's getting bad," he explained.

"What do you mean?" Yen was dubious about his intentions.

"Well, my wife used to call me a hoarder, but it's not that. I keep things I think I might need someday. I've kept a lot of newspapers and magazines in the living room because I go back and re-read them occasionally. I save a lot of plastic takeout containers because they're great for keeping leftovers in, and then I don't have to buy any. And I have a lot of cans and bottles in the basement because I like to collect them. I like the different labels on the bottles, but I also like to try the different beers from all over the world."

"So, what do you want me to do?" she asked skeptically.

"I don't want you to touch the stuff in the basement, but I need help cleaning the house. The dust is getting pretty bad."

"Yes, I can help with that." Yen was still nervous about what he might be up to, but if it truly was as simple as cleaning the house, she could do that. She'd do almost anything to stay on his good side. She actually enjoyed dusting and vacuuming, and often sang while she cleaned her own house.

Walt began bringing Yen out of the dungeon every day and into the house to help him sort through the piles of papers and magazines. She found herself looking forward to that time because it gave her a chance to see something other than the concrete walls of the bunker.

Yen took her time organizing the clutter in Walt's home. She told him she was trying to be thorough. Realistically, she thought if she could maintain her usefulness, maybe he wouldn't kill her or allow his important friends to rape her. Having her gang raped by his friends was a threat he lauded over her, time and time again. He seemed to sense her fear at being raped by more men than just Walt and used that against her.

They started in the kitchen, where they threw away enough old takeout containers and plastic utensils to fill three garbage bags.

"Where are the other women that live here?" Yen boldly asked on her first day of cleaning. "Will they be helping us?"

"No, they're not allowed in the kitchen," Walt said. "They stay in another part of the house, but don't you worry about them. You won't ever see them."

Once the kitchen was made presentable, they proceeded to the living room. Yen questioned whether the abundance of magazines and newspapers piled on the floor and furniture posed a fire hazard. She had never seen so much clutter.

Occasionally, Walt would have the television on while Yen cleaned. She would slow down a bit, hoping to watch whatever show was on. It didn't matter what was playing—sports, a game show, a movie— Anything that reminded her of the outside world was precious to her.

When she began working in the living room, she realized she might have an opportunity to escape and looked for a chance to bolt out the front door. Walt kept it locked with an old-fashioned chain, but maybe there would come a time when he forgot to slide the chain into the keeper. She tried to be as subtle as possible, her eyes glancing between Walt and the door, but he must have suspected that she might make a run for it. He would either stay within an arm's length of her, or he would stand in front of the door with his arms crossed over his chest like a sentry.

He watched her like a hawk as she sorted, cleaned and dusted.

Even with her avenue of escape cut off, she was grateful to be upstairs with the filtered sunlight. Curtains were shut tight in the kitchen and the living room, but bits of light seeped in, and she sucked up every drop of it.

As she sorted through the mail, Yen looked carefully to see if any of the mail listed addresses. She was hoping to find something that would tell her where she was.

Unfortunately, there was no mail that listed a street address in any of the piles.

What she didn't know was that Walt was savvy enough to have gotten rid of any mail with his street address—the envelopes for the junk mail addressed to him were thrown away, with the contents piled in the living room and bills were filed in his home office. She would never see that room.

He had been careful about not leaving envelopes out in the open and took care of them as soon as they arrived in his mailbox.

As she sorted through the piles, Yen would slowly look over the newspapers and magazines—all purchased at the store, so there were no addresses imprinted on the labels—trying to find reasons to keep them. If there weren't any noteworthy articles in them, she would suggest tossing them, but not until after she could assure Walt that the publications were not worth saving.

They went through the reading material one by one. Walt insisted on keeping all the National Geographic and the Playboy magazines, but for the most part, he followed her advice regarding the newspapers and miscellaneous magazines. Walt also wanted to save magazines like the Sports Illustrated Swimsuit Edition, but it didn't matter to Yen. He could keep the whole damn houseful of junk for all she cared because, to Yen, the only thing that mattered was the time she spent out of the bunker. It was time she treasured.

She also suggested throwing away the millions of store receipts and junk mail that he'd accumulated.

Although he agreed to get rid of the junk mail (he didn't need a new roof, was happy with his auto insurance, and wasn't interested in the menu from the newest pizza restaurant), he insisted on keeping the store receipts. It wasn't until she reminded him that, even if he could match up a receipt to an item, almost all of them were so old they were faded and couldn't be read anyway. She convinced him they were no longer valid for any kind of return to the store. Finally, he agreed they had outgrown their usefulness and could be tossed.

It took six months of working an hour or two a day, but finally the house was presentable. The kitchen was now organized, with only a few takeout containers in the cabinet for leftovers. Yen had even scrubbed the stove and refrigerator until they shined.

The mile-high piles of paper scattered throughout the living room were gone. The magazines and newspapers Walt wanted to keep were placed in plastic bins and labeled, while the rest were thrown in the garbage. Walt thanked Yen. He was pleased that the furniture, floors, and kitchen counters were once again visible.

He should have left it all covered, Yen thought to herself. *This house is right out of the 1970s, with orange Formica countertops and green indoor/outdoor carpeting.*

After Yen had finished the sorting, cleaning, dusting, and vacuuming, Walt left her in the dungeon and wouldn't let her return to the house. Now that her "job" was done, Yen was concerned. What would Walt do with her? Pass her around to his friends? Would he kill her like they do on television shows? Or would he keep her forever, to live in a dungeon and be raped whenever he desired?

A few weeks after she'd finished cleaning his house, Walt came to the dungeon one morning and announced he would be taking her for a ride. The calendar with the usual S, B, and T showed it was May. She'd been in the bunker for nine months.

"Why?" she asked fearfully, her voice barely above a whisper.

"Never mind, my Little Rose. Just head to the tunnel." He stretched his arm towards the opening.

"No," Yen said. "Not until you tell me where I'm going."

Walt looked at her with an icy stare but didn't answer her.

"Are you going to kill me?" Yen bit her lip in an attempt to stop the tears that were building in her eyes.

"What? No, I'm not going to kill you. Are you crazy? Why would I do that?"

"Then where are you taking me?"

"I'm letting you go, Little Rose."

Yen stared at Walt for a moment, not sure she heard him correctly. She let out a breath she didn't realize she'd been holding. "You're letting me go?"

"Yes, I am. I've got to take a couple of trips in the next few months, and I can't leave you here by yourself. Just get your ass into the tunnel, will you?"

He seemed to be losing patience with her questions, and the last thing she wanted was to make him angry. Yen almost ran up the stepladder as best she could, while holding the waistband of the too-large sweatpants with one hand. He'd given her a clothes pin to cinch the waistline tighter, but it wasn't very effective because it had a tendency to pop off.

I can't believe it. He's really letting me go? She hoped he was telling the truth.

Yen led the way into the tunnel, crawling as fast as she could in the darkness. The clothes pin had fallen off as she made her way through the tunnel, so she was forced to hold on to the sweatpants with one hand while she clumsily used her other hand for balance. She anxiously waited at the other end for Walt to unlock the doors to the basement.

Once he had her in the newly cleaned living room, he pulled a blindfold out of his pants pocket. He reached towards her to place it over her eyes.

"Please don't put that over my eyes," Yen begged. The idea of not being able to see what he was doing or where he was standing seemed frightening to Yen.

"I don't want you to see where I live when we leave here. You either wear the blindfold or I take you back to the bunker."

"No, I don't want to go back there. Please don't make me go back to the bunker."

As much as Yen disliked the idea of being blindfolded, she did not want to argue and risk her chance at freedom even more. "All right. Go ahead and put it on."

After a quick ride in the car with Walt, the car came to a stop. Yen heard the engine stop running. He had turned off the car. "Don't you dare go to the cops. Do you understand me?"

"Yes, I hear you. I won't say a word." She was close to tears at the uncertainty of what was happening.

"I know where you live, Little Rose, and I can go after you or someone in your family very easily."

She had no way of knowing that was an idle threat. He couldn't have known where she lived because she had not been carrying identification when she was kidnapped, and she hadn't told him anything about her home life. Still, she shuddered at his words.

"I promise. I won't tell," Yen said.

Yen listened intently as his car door opened and closed. She felt the rush of air on her right side as he opened her door. She could feel him grab the knot of the blindfold at the back of her head and yank it off.

She looked over his shoulder, trying to understand what was happening and where she was. It took only a moment for her to realize she was at the bus station. Walt grabbed her by the elbow and pulled her out of the car. Before he let her go, he pressed a $50 bill into her hand.

Without another word, Walt closed the passenger side door, turned away, and got into the driver's seat. Yen sprinted into the building as if the devil himself was behind her.

A kind, older woman let Yen borrow her cell phone. She called her husband, barely able to get the words out as he broke into tears at the sound of her voice. In a matter of minutes, he arrived at the bus station to drive her home.

After a tearful reunion with her family, Yen proceeded to do exactly what she had promised Walt she wouldn't do. She went to the police.

CHAPTER THIRTEEN

A few months before Yen was released from the bunker, Steve "Mac" MacIntosh received a promotion to the position of investigator when Tony Donatella finally retired. The move into the Criminal Investigations Division meant he would be home more often, something that his wife, Alayna, appreciated and looked forward to.

Mac had been at his desk when he heard the call dispatched over the radio. "Return to the PD," the dispatcher said to one of their police officers on the road, "on an assist to a citizen for a kidnapping complaint."

Mac quickly logged into the county 911 dispatch computer program to check the notes on the call. He'd heard it correctly. A woman named Yen Nguyen was in their lobby, waiting to talk to a police officer. According to the notes, she was reporting she had been held captive for almost a year in an underground bunker and raped daily by a man she described as being in his sixties.

Unbelievably, it sounded like the same situation Gabrielle Reyes had reported the year before. Mac's heart raced as he picked up the phone to call the 911 dispatcher.

"You can cancel the officer that's returning to the PD to take that call," Mac told the dispatcher. "I'll talk to the victim."

Mac proceeded into the lobby to meet with the victim. He found a small Asian woman and an Asian man sitting next to her on the cold metal bench. As Mac extended his hand to shake theirs, he introduced himself.

"I'm Investigator MacIntosh, and I'll be talking with you today."

"I'm Yen, and this is my husband, Tran," the woman said quietly.

"If you'd like to come with me, we'll go somewhere more comfortable to talk."

Mac led the way to the conference room and held the door open. "Please, come in."

With his hand extended, he invited them to sit at the long table. Yen looked up and noticed the camera hanging from the ceiling in the corner of the room. "Are you taping this?" she asked.

"No, not unless you want me to," Mac said.

"No, please don't. I don't want it on tape." Yen shook her head vehemently.

"That's fine. I don't have to turn it on. I will take notes, though."

"Yes, that's fine. It's just that this is very hard to talk about. I'm very ashamed. He raped me every day." Tran reached for her hand and squeezed as the tears ran down her cheek.

"Listen to me," Mac looked her square in the eyes and spoke firmly. "What he did to you is not your fault. He is an evil man, and he did horrible things to you. None of that is your fault. I know this isn't easy, but if you can, I need you to tell me what happened. I know it will be difficult, but the more you can tell me, the better our chances will be to find this guy and arrest him."

Over the next two hours, Yen told a similar story as Daniella had relayed. An older man named Walt had held them both in an underground bunker, raped them every day, and made them write an S, B, or T on a calendar. He threatened their families to keep them in line and made his brags that he had important law enforcement friends from the local to the federal levels. Even their descriptions of the bunker, bathtub, mattress, and graffiti matched.

Both women also reported that Walt had not had sex with them for several days prior to their release. Mac felt sure this was so there wouldn't be any DNA that could be traced back to this Walt character.

There were, however, a few differences. Where Daniella did not report any violence, Yen told of Walt smacking her a couple times. She admitted she was still having pain in her left ear because he'd hit her there twice. It was a constant reminder from the very first day he'd kidnapped her. Clearly, his use of violence was escalating. That was not a good sign.

She was also allowed out of the bunker to clean his house and to help him organize piles and piles of magazines, newspapers, and receipts. Daniella wasn't allowed out at all until her release.

Still, there was no question it was the same guy that held both women captive. To Mac, Yen's story meant this Walt guy seemed to be getting more comfortable kidnapping women. But was he more brazen with Yen? Was it because he thought she was too afraid to go to the cops or simply because he was getting overly confident and cocky?

After the interview with Yen, Mac pulled out the notes from Daniella's kidnapping. He had kept them close by on his desk and reread them every now and again.

He always hoped that someday he'd find something he might have missed.

He read through the paperwork again, even though he'd done it so many times, he knew them by heart. Unfortunately, he couldn't see anything that would help identify Walt. There were just no leads on his identity or his address.

Daniella and Yen had been told by Walt not to go to the police or else he would kill someone in their families. Mac knew there could be other victims who listened to the threats and never reported their kidnapping to the police. If Walt's threats were to be believed, these two women were taking a chance by reporting their kidnapping.

Mac was aimlessly driving around, his mind filled with details of a woman reported missing by her family that morning. She was a known drug user and occasionally disappeared for a few days at a time but had never been gone this long. They last had contact with her the week before.

Mac wondered, could she be a victim of the man known to kidnap women and hold them in an underground bunker?

It had been two years since Yen Nguyen told Mac an older man named Walt, who had white hair, a closely cropped beard and oversized glasses, had kidnapped and raped her. He usually wore khaki pants and polo shirts. Unfortunately, that could be almost any older man.

Mac's attempts to find the kidnapper were futile. He still had Gabriella's and Yen's files on his desk as a constant reminder, but he needed something concrete, something definitive, that would lead him to Walt. Without an address, a last name, or a witness that could identify him, the hopes of finding the kidnapper were slim.

As Mac turned the corner onto Battle Creek Road, he suddenly had to swerve to avoid an older, tan car that was parked on the side of the road, the tail end still in the driving lane. An older man, wearing khakis and a light blue polo shirt, was in front of the car with his back to the road. He was picking up a bottle from the side of the road.

Mac shook his head, thinking how foolish the man was, for the sake of a plain glass bottle.

Chapter Fourteen

Emily Tuttle slowly ambled her way down Main Street, with her eyes focused skyward through the raindrops. She occasionally bumped into people, poles and outdoor cafe tables but rarely broke her gaze from the clouds.

"Those butterflies are awesome," she said to no one in particular, a lopsided grin exposing her teeth. She reached up as if to grab a butterfly but pulled her empty hand back to rest against her chest. The butterflies were nothing more than an LSD-induced figment of her imagination.

As Emily walked past the Family Food Market, an older man exited the store and almost ran into her. She never broke her slow stride or her skyward stare. The man stopped in his tracks.

"Hey," he said. "Are you okay?"

"Aren't they beautiful?" she asked.

"What are you talking about? What's beautiful?" the man asked, as he followed her gaze and looked around. He couldn't see what she was looking at. He snapped his fingers in front of her face. She gave no reaction to the sudden, sharp noise or the rain that continued to pour down, plastering her bangs to her forehead.

"The butterflies. They're beautiful. Look at all the pretty colors! Don't you see them?"

"Um, yeah, sure. Sure, I see them. They are beautiful." He cast an evil leer in her direction. Walt realized he was looking at his next victim. "Would you like a ride? It's pouring out here, and you're getting soaked."

When she didn't respond to his question, Walt put his arm around her back and led her to the parking lot. He opened the passenger side door and eased her into his car. He pulled the seatbelt taut over her hips then cupped her breast with the palm of his hand. She gave no reaction to being fondled. As he pulled out of the parking lot, he was already feeling the excitement, knowing what lay ahead.

It had been a long three years, almost to the day, since Yen had been released. During that time, his son, Gregory, had been living with him for over a year after he fell from a roof and was injured. Walt had been anxiously awaiting the day when he could find a woman to keep in the bunker again. It appeared the wait was over.

Once he drove her to his house, he led her to the basement toward his secret hideaway. She offered no resistance as he unlocked the doors, led her through, and re-locked the doors behind them.

They stood in front of the darkened tunnel. Walt, holding the lit flashlight over her head, told her to crawl into the hole and she'd get a big surprise.

"Ooh," she said. "What kind of surprise?" The effects of the drug were still very much in her system, continuing to make her loopy.

"Have you ever heard of Alice in Wonderland? You know how she went down a rabbit hole? Well, this is kind of like that."

"Whoa! That sounds cool!"

"All you have to do," said Walt, "is turn around and crawl backwards into the tunnel."

"Oh, wow! That's silly." The young woman giggled. She did as Walt asked and crawled backward into the tunnel, her laughs echoing off the close walls.

Walt warned her that at the end of the tunnel, she would find a stepladder. Once on solid ground in the bunker, the woman spun around, looking at the strange room.

"What is this, some kind of room you hide in to get away from the wife and kids?" She laughed at her own joke.

"Yeah, sure. I hide in here. Come this way and let me show you the other room." Walt took hold of her arm and led her into the room with the mattress. He turned on the floor lamp on the way.

The drugs in her system slowed her ability to react, and Walt took advantage of that. He pushed her down onto the mattress, her body falling half on and half off the mattress. Before her brain could process the information, Walt had deftly taken her pants off and was squeezing her breasts.

Before her drug-addled brain could comprehend, Walt forcefully raped her, as he always did with his captives as soon as they were brought to the bunker. He was rather rough with her in his haste, although Emily smiled and actively took part, as if she was feeling euphoric and enjoyed it.

He had never been with a woman that was high on drugs before, but he discovered he could be forceful, sadistic and even cruel, and they both seemed to respond well to the harsher treatment. That opened up a whole new world for Walt.

"What's your name?" he asked. He stood over her as she lay naked on the thin mattress.

"Emily. What's yours?"

"My name's Walt. How old are you?"

"I'm twenty-six. Where are we? This place looks really weird."

"This is my special place where you're going to live for a while."

"I'm not going to live here. I have my own apartment." With the passage of time since she'd taken the LSD and certainly the shock of her situation, it appeared the effects of the drug were beginning to wear off.

"You *are* going to live here, but don't worry. I'll make sure you're well taken care of. I'll feed you, you'll be able to take a bath and brush your teeth when I let you, and you even have a radio for listening to music.

All you have to do is have sex with me whenever I want it. Doesn't that sound nice?"

"Are you crazy? I don't want to live here, and I don't want to have sex with you."

"You've already had sex with me, Emily, and it was pretty good. You're quite a little vixen, you know that?" Emily shivered at the sly look he gave her.

Emily looked down and gasped at her naked body. She attempted to fully sit up, but then clearly realized her hands were handcuffed to the wall behind her. She pulled at the restraints, cutting into the skin on her wrists. "What's wrong with you?" she yelled. "You're out of your freaking mind if you think I'm staying here! Let me go!"

"I can't do that. Now, I'm going to fix us some dinner, and if you're a good girl, I'll take off one of the handcuffs so you can eat. I'll see you later, my Little Flower."

Her screams filled the air as Walt locked the door at the end of the tunnel, leaving his new captive cold, naked, and chained to the wall.

CHAPTER FIFTEEN

Gradually, Walt introduced Emily to life in the underground bunker. On the first day, he had shown her the toilet where she was to pee into a bucket. She had already seen the stained mattress she was supposed to sleep on and found it to be disgusting. But it was still better than sleeping on the cold, hard cement floor.

Over the next several days, he explained how to use the tub where she was to bathe using only a couple inches of cold water from the garden hose. He brought her food every day, but on an inconsistent schedule. He showed her the calendar where she would write the standard S for sex, B for bath, or T for brushing her teeth.

When she threatened to escape, he gave Emily the same stories he'd told his other captives, that he was good friends with politicians, celebrities and the chief of police. He told her he was part of an underground sex-slave syndicate that he and these influential men belonged to. Essentially, he explained, it was a club where he was in charge of "training" the women that would please the other members. He even showed her a police badge to prove his alleged affiliation with such men. If she tried to escape, these friends of his would hunt her down.

Missing her family and friends tremendously, Emily spent most of her time in the dungeon thinking of ways to escape but hadn't found any viable solutions. She had crawled through the tunnel countless times, hoping that, just once, Walt would have forgotten to lock the doors after he left. Each time she was disappointed to find the door would not budge.

Then she came up with a plan that might work. After being held in the bunker for about a month, Emily asked Walt if she could telephone her parents. She said they were probably worried about her, and she wanted to let them know she was alive.

Walt agreed to let her contact her parents, but only on the condition she send a letter, and she must tell them she was in drug rehab. Grudgingly, Emily agreed. It obviously wasn't the truth, but it was better than nothing.

Emily thought if she could deliver a coded message to them, if she wrote something out of the ordinary, perhaps her parents could read between the lines and realize she was trying to alert them that something was wrong.

Emily did just that. She began the letter by calling them Betty and Paul, rather than Mom and Dad; she referred to being in drug rehab again—she'd never been before; and she wrote that she really missed her cat Hercules. Hercules was a favorite stuffed dog she played with as a child.

Of course, Walt read the letter before he mailed it. He had no way to pick up on the hidden messages she had incorporated into the note, so he allowed her to send it as is. All she could do now was hope that her parents picked up on the inconsistencies in the letter and would start searching for her.

Emily had always been a bit of a free spirit. Her best friend used to tell her she would have been a great hippie and should have been born in the sixties. Because of that free spirit, Emily had always had a healthy sex life with both men and women and was not shy about experimenting with toys, styles, or multiple partners. But that had been her choice, and the idea of being forced into having sex with this guy was not something she catered to.

As the weeks rolled into months, Walt became progressively rougher with their sex by inflicting pain on her. He usually slapped or pinched her, which were things Emily detested.

One day, he came into the bunker with a lit cigar. He forced her to lie on her stomach while they had sex, and he touched the lit cigar to her back as he pushed into her. Emily screamed in pain, twisting from side to side in a failed attempt to push him away.

Her screams seemed to excite Walt even more. He gave a loud grunt as he exploded inside her. Beads of sweat fell from his forehead onto her back and ran down her side.

Once he finished, he quickly dressed and left the bunker without saying another word. The tears flowed from her eyes in a steady stream. The burn on her back hurt like hell, and the smell of burned flesh filled the air.

He only burned her that one time, but once was enough. The burn had abscessed and caused incredible pain every time Emily twisted her torso, maneuvered onto her side while lying on the mattress, or when Walt forced her to lie on her back for sex.

Emily had been in the bunker for six months under Walt's captivity, and the abscess from the cigar burn a week prior was getting worse. The infection had spread so that a good portion of her lower back was red and warm to the touch, while the burn itself was now a large pus-filled area. It had grown to be at least twice the size of the original burn. Emily was in a tremendous amount of pain.

Walt had been so busy satisfying his needs that he didn't realize the burn had abscessed so badly. When he finally saw the damage, he panicked. He knew the time had come when he would have to let her go.

For the next three days, Walt abstained from having sex with Emily. He told her it was because he didn't want to hurt her further, when in reality, it was so he wouldn't leave any forensic evidence. When he released her, he would warn her not to go to the police, but on the odd chance that she ignored his warning, he didn't want the authorities to find his DNA in her or on her.

During that time, Emily became lethargic as the fever took hold. She spent most of her time lying as still as possible on the mattress. When she had to move, it left her in tears. A trip to the toilet in the other room was a painful and exhausting ordeal, so Walt allowed her to move the thin, tattered mattress into the same room as the toilet. At least she wouldn't have as far to walk.

On the morning of the third day, Walt told her he was letting her go and gave her clean clothes to change into. He gently helped her through the tunnel, into the house and outdoors as she kept her eyes closed from the pain. His mistake was in not blindfolding her as he did his previous victims.

She knew as he walked her to the car that she might have an opportunity to identify her captor by something notable in the surroundings. When she spotted the car, she recalled her father's stories and the photos he'd shown her of his very first car—it looked like the same model, a 1984 Dodge Daytona.

Walt led her to the car and opened the front passenger door to let her in. With tears filling her eyes, Emily asked if she could lie down in the back seat. It would hurt too much to sit in the front and lean against the back of the seat. Walt hesitated but agreed.

"Where do you want to be dropped off? Your apartment or someplace else?" His voice was quiet, without the usual cockiness.

"My parents' house," she answered. She gave Walt the address.

He drove her to within a block of her parents' house and let her out.

"Don't forget, my Little Rose, if you go to the police, I will find out. Remember, the chief is a very close friend, and he tells me everything." Walt left her leaning against a light pole, her arms wrapped around the cold metal for support. He got in the car and sped off.

Emily had no phone, no money, and no energy, but a lot of pain. After several minutes, a young man of about sixteen years of age was passing by and stopped to ask if she was all right. "You don't look so good," he said. "Are you okay?"

"No, actually, I'm not. Do you have a cell phone I could borrow?"

"Yeah, sure." He pulled a phone from his jeans pocket and handed it to her. Emily quickly dialed the number she'd had committed to memory since she was a little girl. "Mom? Oh, my God, Mom! Can you pick me up?... Please?... I know, but I can explain. I didn't run away, someone kidnapped me... No, I'm not lying.... Please come get me... Okay. Thank you. I'm in front of the Punjab Corner Market.... Thank you.... And Mom? Can you hurry, please?"

Emily handed the phone back to the young man and thanked him. After hearing her side of the conversation, he offered to help her. "Listen, if you want, I'll stay with you until your mom gets here."

"That's okay. I'm alright, just in a lot of pain. My mom is on her way. We live down the street, so she should be here in a few minutes." She was gritting her teeth as she spoke.

The teenager watched Emily wrap her arms tighter around the pole. "Really, I don't mind. Geez, it sounds like you've gone through a lot. I'll stay until your mom gets here and make sure you're okay."

"Okay. Thank you. I appreciate you, even though it might not seem like it right now."

The young man stayed with Emily, making small talk. She was in too much pain to converse more than a few words at a time. Later on, Emily would regret not getting the man's name. She was extremely grateful to him for standing with her for that bit of time, making her feel like the kidnapping was behind her and she was now free. Maybe someday, she thought, she'd be able to find out who he was and thank him.

Within minutes, Emily's parents pulled up to the curb and jumped out of the car. Her mother reached her first and wrapped her arms around Emily's shoulders in a tight embrace. Emily let out a soft scream. Alarmed, her mother pulled back and looked at Emily, frightened and confused that she might have hurt her daughter.

After a tearful reunion with her parents on the sidewalk, Emily begged to go to the hospital emergency room to have the abscess treated. They dropped her father off at home, and Emily and her mother continued on to the hospital.

The doctor lanced the abscess and also conducted a rape kit. Unfortunately, he found no forensic evidence, either on her person or the clean clothes Walt had given her that morning. Walt's decision to not have sex with her before her release had paid off— for him at least.

CHAPTER SIXTEEN

A few days later, after the antibiotics kicked in and she was better able to move, Emily went to the police department to file a report against Walt. A man in a crisp shirt and tie came to talk with her.

"Hi," he said, as he extended his hand. "My name is Sergeant Steve MacIntosh."

Emily took his hand. "Are you a cop? How come you're not wearing a uniform?"

"I'm a sergeant, but I'm also an investigator, and I'm in charge of the investigators. If you'd like to follow me, we'll go to a separate room to talk privately."

Mac received a promotion to sergeant only a few months before. Although he would now carry more responsibilities as head of the Criminal Investigation Department, he fell into the role easily and found that he enjoyed it.

Mac led Emily to the conference room. "Would you like some water or a cup of coffee?" he said.

"No, thank you. My nerves are already shot. The last thing I need is some caffeine right now." Emily offered a slight smile.

Mac listened intently as Emily spoke of being kidnapped approximately six months before and of being held in an underground bunker. She described the bunker as having graffiti on the walls of the two rooms, with one room being the bathing area, the other being the sleeping area. She told Mac of how her captor raped her daily and referred to her as his "Little Flower" or "Little Rose." She was forced to keep a calendar, recording an S, B or T on the squares with a red crayon.

Mac recognized Emily's story as being very similar to Gabrielle's and Yen's. "Can you describe your kidnapper?" he asked.

"He's about sixty-five or seventy years old, average height, average weight. He wears large glasses that make him look like an owl. And he drives a tan 1984 Dodge Daytona." She repeatedly tapped her finger on the table as she made this point.

"How do you know it's an '84 Dodge Daytona?" Mac was cautiously optimistic about this bit of news. A thirty-six-year-old car should be fairly easy to trace.

"He drove me home in it. Well, almost home. He dropped me off about a block from my parent's house."

"He didn't blindfold you when he brought you home?" Mac asked.

"A blindfold? No, he didn't blindfold me. Why would he do that?"

"There were two other victims that we know of, and they both said they had been blindfolded before he let them go."

"Oh, my God. I thought there might have been other victims. That explains the graffiti on the walls. That's awful." Emily hung her head, remaining quiet for a moment.

With a deep breath, she continued. "Well, he didn't blindfold me, but I think maybe it's because I had my eyes closed when he led me out. He'd burned me on my back with a cigar a couple weeks ago, and it got infected. I was in a lot of pain, and it really hurt to move, so I mostly laid on the mattress in the dungeon and kept my eyes closed because it hurt so much. I think that's when he decided to let me go because the burn was getting worse. Then when he led me out of the house, I mostly still kept my eyes closed, but I opened them just enough to see where we were going. That's when I saw the car parked in front of the house, and that's the car he put me in to drive me home."

"How do you know it was an '84 Dodge Daytona?" asked Mac.

"It was my dad's first car," Emily said, "and he's told us a lot of stories over the years about that car and how he worked several jobs while he was in high school so he could afford to buy it. He used to show us a lot of pictures of the car, too, because he was so proud of it. He said he had to borrow money from his grandfather, but he worked really hard to pay all that money back. I used to hate those stories. Now I'm glad I listened to him."

"Did you happen to recognize the house or see what street it was on?"

"No. I have no idea where it was. I wasn't able to look back at the house as we left because he was at my side and helped me walk to the car. Then, once I got in the car, I had to lie down in the back seat. I couldn't see anything."

"You said he asked you to call him Walt. Did he give you his full name?"

"Nope. He just said to call him Walt, like we were buddies or something. Oh! He also said he had friends in high places, men like the police chief." Emily gave Mac a sideways glance, as if to see how he'd respond.

Mac didn't show a reaction to the statement. As a matter of fact, he'd bet his last paycheck the chief was *not* friends with this low-life sexual predator.

"He let me write a letter to my parents," Emily said. "I needed to let them know I was alive, but I really wanted them to find me. I tried to put some hidden messages in the letter, so they'd know something was wrong, but it didn't work. They told me after I got home that they thought I was high when I wrote it. They never reported me as missing to the police."

"What do you mean, you put 'hidden messages' in the letter? What kind of hidden messages?"

"Well, instead of saying 'Mom and Dad,' I called them by their first names, Betty and Paul. I've never called them that. They were always Mom and Dad. And I asked about my cat, Hercules, but I don't own a cat. Hercules was my favorite stuffed dog I played with as a kid."

"That's pretty clever." Mac nodded his head. "I'm sorry it didn't work, but I give you a lot of credit for thinking of that."

After the interview, Mac went back to the CID office. Investigator James "Coop" Cooper was at his desk, his feet resting against an open drawer while he read a report resting on his lap. "Well, how did it go? Did the victim identify this Walt guy?" he asked. He was familiar with the case after Mac had talked about it so many times in the past.

"No, but she told exactly the same story as the other victims. She described the bunker and her captor to a 'T.' She added one important thing, though. She said he drives a tan 1984 Dodge Daytona."

Mac looked towards Heidi Thompson, the newest investigator. She'd joined their team four months prior. "Heidi, can you do me a favor and see if you can run that car through the Department of Motor Vehicles database? We need to see if we can find that car. I can't believe too many of them are still on the road, so hopefully, we can find it."

"You got it, boss. I'm on it." She put down the report she'd been reading and started pecking at the keys on her computer.

Mac returned to his desk and opened the notebook he'd written notes in during the interview with Emily. Turning to his computer, he began typing the report from the interview. He wanted to record as many of the details as possible while the information was still fresh in his mind.

A few minutes later, Heidi knocked on his door. "I have the results you were looking for. I came back with just one car in the area, but it's a maroon-colored 1984 Dodge Daytona, not a tan color as our victim described."

"This might be a long shot, but I'd like you to go to the registered address for that car and see if it's still maroon. Maybe it's been repainted tan, in which case we may have our first lead."

"You got it, boss," Heidi said.

Mac was disappointed. He was sure they would be able to locate that vehicle. Unfortunately, it was possible it wasn't in the computer system because it might be unregistered, in which case, there would be no record of it. It would now be like looking for a needle in a haystack. They were back to square one, no further ahead than they were a few years ago, with no viable leads.

The best he could do would be to alert road patrol to be on the lookout for a tan 1984 Dodge Daytona.

He would also reach out to police departments in nearby areas and ask them to keep an eye out as well. The officers couldn't stop the car if they spotted it, but they could record the license plate number. Once they had that, they might get an owner's name and address through the motor vehicle website.

Mac sat at his desk, lost in thought. How were they going to catch this guy? They now had three victims and were no closer to identifying him as they were when the first victim came in.

CHAPTER SEVENTEEN

Deshawna Washington was angry. Very angry. Her parents wouldn't let her go to the school dance on Saturday with Jamal because they expected her to babysit her younger siblings while they went out with friends. Deshawna and her family had moved to the area only six months before, and Jamal was one of the first boys she'd met in the new school. She'd had a crush on him since the first time she laid eyes on him and was so happy he'd asked her to the dance.

And now she couldn't go because her parents expected her to babysit. She was tired of always having to ruin her plans for the sake of her little brother and sister. Her parents could go out whenever they wanted, but God forbid Deshawna should ever get to go out. Out of the five kids in the family, Deshawna was the one that got stuck babysitting, Every! Single! Time! That really sucked.

Her older brother, Antony, was lucky. At twenty, he was the oldest. He was away at college so he could go out with his friends any time he wanted. He didn't have to worry about getting stuck babysitting.

Next was Naomi, who was seventeen and a senior in high school. She never had to babysit because, on the rare occasion when their parents asked her to, Naomi would tell them she was going to the library to study, even when she wasn't. Deshawna knew that sometimes Naomi lied to their parents and was going to parties instead. Even on school nights. But when Deshawna tattled on Naomi, their parents didn't push the issue because Naomi got good grades, had a part-time job at the mall, and would be leaving for college next year.

That left Deshawna to babysit for Nyla, who was twelve, and Jaden, who would be ten in a couple months. Deshawna didn't really mind babysitting Nyla. Even though Nyla was a few years younger than Deshawna, they usually got along well. They both enjoyed shopping for clothes, experimenting with makeup, and trying different hairstyles. She was a good kid and helped Deshawna with their younger brother.

Jaden, however, was a pain, but that's only because he liked to bug Deshawna, especially when she was talking on the phone with her friends, doing her homework, or playing video games. Jaden would purposely interrupt whenever she was busy with something and pester her until she stopped what she was doing to play with him. He had ADHD, and even with medication, he had trouble controlling his hyperactivity, which didn't help the situation.

Deshawna understood that, but she still wished he'd stop bugging her.

At sixteen, Deshawna, being the middle child, was expected to be available for babysitting whenever her parents went out. It didn't matter that she might have plans. Nobody ever asked. Everyone just assumed she was available.

Deshawna tried to explain to her mother that a cute boy in school had asked her to the dance on Saturday, but her mother didn't want to hear it. Her parents had plans. Deshawna was to stay home with Nyla and Jaden, and that's all there was to it.

So, before she got in trouble for sassing back to her mother, Deshawna left the house to go for a walk until she could cool off. She stormed out the front door, letting it slam closed behind her, and started walking at a fast pace, almost a run.

After an hour of walking, Deshawna looked around at her surroundings but couldn't place where she was. It seemed to be a fairly busy road, only two lanes wide, but the cars were traveling fast. She decided the best thing to do was to turn around and head back in the direction she came from. Eventually, she would recognize a landmark, she was sure.

But turning around meant the setting sun was directly in front of her. Without her sunglasses, it was hard to see. It helped to hold her hand over her eyes like a visor, but her arm got tired after a while. Now she was angry, tired, hungry, blinded and lost. Great. Just great.

Deshawna stopped to look around. Nothing looked familiar yet. Suddenly, a car turned into a driveway directly in front of her. She jumped back, startled by the sudden appearance of the vehicle that now blocked her path. A man got out of the driver's door and called to her.

"Hey! You look lost. Are you okay?" the man asked.

"Um, no, I'm not okay. I am lost. What road is this?"

The man didn't answer the question. "Do you need a lift? I'd be happy to give you a ride home."

Deshawna studied him. He was an older man with large glasses and a wide smile. He looked friendly. "Yeah, I'd like that, if you don't mind. I didn't realize I'd walked this far."

"Sure, I can help you. I'll take you home." He opened the passenger side door so Deshawna could get in the car. He reached for the seatbelt and held it out for her.

"Don't forget to buckle up. We don't want you getting hurt." He shut her door and got in the driver's seat.

"What street do you live on?" the man asked.

Deshawna gave him her address. "I don't know where it is from here, though. I'm kind of new to the area. We only moved here about six months ago, so I don't know my way around yet."

They headed in the direction Deshawna had been walking. The man asked a lot of questions about her family. She was more than willing to tell the man about how she was stuck babysitting her younger sister and brother, even though she'd rather go to the dance with Jamal. She had been angry and needed the time and space a long walk offered in order to calm down. That's why she ended up walking so far from home, she explained.

As she talked, Deshawna looked out the windows, trying to get her bearings. After a few minutes, she began to recognize some of the buildings. "Oh, my gosh. I know where I am now. The mall is right up here, right?"

"Yes, it is," the man said.

"Cool. All you have to do is turn right here, and I can tell you how to go from there... Hey, you were supposed to turn back there. You need to go back to that last street. Hey! You missed the turn!"

The man stared straight ahead, a smile lifting the corners of his mouth.

"What are you doing? Stop! Stop the car!" Deshawna was yelling at the man, but he wasn't listening. He continued to drive farther and farther away from her home.

Deshawna thrashed in the front seat, pounding her fists on the dashboard and pulling on the door handle. The door would not open. What she didn't know was that Walt had disabled the latch mechanism on the passenger-side door, to prevent his victims from escaping.

She watched in horror as the man turned onto different roads she was unfamiliar with. She lost her sense of direction and didn't know where she was.

He finally pulled into a driveway. Tall bushes on either side of the driveway hid the opening until the car eased through the slight clearing between the bushes.

Deshawna tugged on the door handle, but it still wouldn't open. The man came around to the passenger side door and opened it from the outside. He quickly grabbed her arm underneath the armpit and lifted her from the car.

"What are you doing? You're hurting me!" Deshawna's eyes were wide with panic.

The man led her towards the front door of a wide ranch home. "You're going to be my guest for a while." With one hand still firmly gripping Deshawna's arm, he used his free hand to turn the doorknob. He pushed her through the door and into his lair.

CHAPTER EIGHTEEN

Never in her wildest dreams could Deshawna have imagined being held in an underground cinder-block room by an older man who forced her to have sex with him every day.

The first day of captivity was the worst day of her life. The man she now knew as Walt had literally dragged her through his house and into a tunnel. She was now living in two dark, windowless, musty rooms he referred to as a "bunker."

Within minutes of entering the bunker, he had defiled her. At sixteen years old, she had always thought her first time would be something romantic, shared between her and the man she loved. Now he'd taken that dream away from her.

Walt came into the bunker every day and forced himself on her. For that, she hated him. She hated everything about him for stealing her innocence, her virginity, her child-like dream of falling in love with Prince Charming.

Occasionally, he would slap her behind in keeping with the rough sex that he enjoyed. She hadn't even been spanked as a child and found the violence he inflicted on her to be a way of making a terrible situation even worse.

Deshawna was strong, though. She knew she couldn't physically fight him, but emotionally, she wouldn't let him win. She quickly learned to mentally distance herself from the situation while Walt was raping her. She would picture herself far away—she would take herself on a picnic, to the beach, or to a dance with Jamal.

She got the idea from the historical fiction books she loved to read. During the olden days, women who were in arranged marriages and not in love with their husbands would simply concentrate on something more pleasant while their husbands satisfied themselves. Most women didn't enjoy sex, the novels claimed. Rather, they laid on the bed while the men did what they had to do. Women had no choice but to put up with it because, in those days, it was believed that the woman's "duty" was to have as many children as possible.

Deshawna missed her family terribly. She even missed her annoying little brother more than she thought she would. She would give anything to feel his hand tapping on her shoulder as he begged, "Come play with me, Dee. Come on. Let's play some video games."

She really missed walking to the mall with her sister, the smell of rain on a summer day, and the warmth of the sun shining on her face. She missed cutting the grass. It had been one of her favorite things to do and had become her job at home.

Deshawna had been in the bunker for about two months when she saw, according to the calendar Walt gave her to post an S, B or T on, today was Jaden's birthday. When Walt entered the bunker, he found her curled up on the mattress, crying.

"What's the matter, my Little Flower? Do you feel okay?" he asked.

"I miss my family so much." She spoke so softly, Walt had difficulty hearing her.

"It's my little brother's birthday today."

"Oh," said Walt.

"I know they're going to have cake and presents. Everyone in the family will be there... except me." Deshawna buried her head in her arms. She didn't want Walt to see her crying, but she couldn't help it. The thought of the family having a party while she was being held captive in the bunker broke her heart.

Walt finished with their daily sex routine and left, only to return to the bunker about an hour later.

Deshawna was still lying on the thin mattress, curled into the fetal position.

"I brought you something." Walt extended his hand to her.

She looked up to see a cupcake in his hand. The candle was burning as brightly as Walt's grin.

Deshawna looked from the cupcake to Walt and back again. Her chin dropped, but no words would come. She was stunned. Did he not understand? It was her family she missed, not the damned cupcake!

Walt saw her reaction and must have realized he made a mistake. He set the cupcake on the overturned milk crate and left the bunker.

Walt had kidnapped Deshawna in October. Now, six long months later, she continually daydreamed about the day when she might escape. For the umpteenth time, she begged Walt to let her go.

"I promise I won't tell anyone. Please let me go. I just want to see my family again. You have no idea how much I miss them. I hate being stuck in here. I've always been an outdoors person, and I really miss that. I miss seeing the sun, the trees, and the flowers." The tears ran down her cheeks as she pleaded for her freedom.

Walt hesitated for a moment and gave her a puzzled look. "What if..."

Deshawna waited for him to finish, but he said nothing further. He just looked at her, his brow furrowed, as if he was thinking.

"What do you mean, 'what if'?" she asked.

"Never mind. I'll be back." And with that, Walt climbed up the ladder and out of the bunker.

Two hours later, he was back in the bunker to find Deshawna lying on the thin mattress, her back against the wall. She gave him an angry look.

"What do you want?" He'd already had sex with her that afternoon, so she figured he wasn't after that.

"How would you like to go to a bar with me? Just for a little while," he said.

Deshawna spun around to sit on her knees. "Are you serious?"

"Yes, my Little Rose, I am. They have karaoke at this bar I know on Thursday nights, and I like to go to listen. But you have to promise not to try anything funny.

If you try to run away from me, I'll have the chief of police bring you back. I've told you before, he's a good friend of mine and will do anything I ask."

Deshawna believed his threat. Many times, he had told her about the "friends" he had in high places. She had no reason to doubt his word.

"I'll be good, I promise. I won't run away. Can we please go? Please?" She was hopping up and down, still on her knees.

Deshawna hadn't realized Walt was carrying a plastic bag from Walmart. He tossed it at her. "Here," he said, "put these on."

She looked in the bag and pulled out a new pair of jeans, a sweatshirt, socks, underwear, and a bra. "You can wear that stuff tonight. As soon as you're dressed, my Little Rose, we'll go."

Excited to be leaving the confines of the dungeon, Deshawna got dressed in record time. "You'll have to wear your own sneakers. I didn't get you a new pair because I wasn't sure about the size."

"That's fine. Thank you." She was being overly nice, remembering her grandmother's words, "You get more flies with honey than with vinegar." Getting out of the bunker, even for a few hours, was more valuable to her than having to swallow her pride and be polite to her kidnapper.

What she didn't expect was for Walt to pull a large bandana from his back pocket and put it over her eyes. She resisted at first but finally relented after Walt told her she had to wear the blindfold, or they wouldn't go. She was very disappointed she wouldn't be able to look at the scenery outside the car windows, but she knew he couldn't make her wear it inside the bar. That would draw too much unwanted attention. At least, she hoped she wouldn't have to wear it at the bar.

With the bandana covering her eyes, Walt helped her into the car. On the way to the bar, he told her he was intentionally driving the long way around, just in case she was trying to memorize the left and right turns he took. He said he didn't want her figuring out where they were. What normally would have been a ten-minute drive took twenty-five.

Deshawna knew they must have arrived at the bar when she felt the car rock back and forth, as if Walt was driving on a heavily rutted dirt parking lot. After the car stopped, he reached behind her head and untied the bandana.

"Remember, my Little Rose, you promised me you wouldn't try anything funny. I expect you to keep that promise because if you don't, you know what will happen."

"I will. No funny business. I promise." Her eyes were open wide with excitement. She looked at her surroundings, appreciating the bright neon lights shining from inside the bar windows advertising the different brands of beer the bar apparently offered. The stars in the nighttime sky above were twinkling brightly in the cloudless sky. It was beautiful.

The bar itself looked to be a log-covered building surrounded by trees and bushes on three of the four sides of the large lot. She couldn't see if there were any nearby buildings through the thick foliage. Deshawna looked, but there didn't appear to be a name for the bar on the facade or in neon in the window. That was disappointing. If she ever got out of Walt's grasp, she wanted to note the name of the bar, or at the very least, any recognizable landmarks.

As she spun in a circle trying to find anything identifiable, she saw a large, wooden sign at the entrance to the parking lot facing the street. A single spotlight shone on one side of the sign, but the other side was dark. She'd be willing to bet, the name of the bar must be on the sign.

Deshawna was so busy looking at the surrounding area and the stars that she didn't look down to see the potholes and ruts littering the parking lot. Before she could catch herself, she stepped into a deep hole and began to fall. If it weren't for Walt's tight grip on her arm, she would have landed on the ground.

"Easy, now, Little Rose. Are you all right?" Walt asked, as he held her up by one arm.

"Yes, I'm fine. I guess I was so busy looking at the stars that I didn't see the hole in the ground. Thank you, Walt." It was the first time she had ever called him by name. Saying it made her sick to her stomach, but she had to play nice if he were to trust her.

Walt led the way through the door, holding tightly to Deshawna's elbow. He stopped at the bar, said hello to the bartender, and bought a draft beer for himself and a soda for her. They found a table in the back of the bar, where the already-darkened room had even less lighting.

Deshawna noted the fact that Walt and the bartender exchanged greetings using their first names. Her captor was obviously a regular at the bar.

Walt seemed to be enjoying himself. He would occasionally glance at her and smile. Playing nice, she would be sure to return the smiles. Deshawna bobbed her head to the music as the karaoke singers belted out their songs. She wanted to show him she was enjoying herself, but more importantly, she aimed to prove she could be trusted to keep her promise.

Realistically, Deshawna was looking for an opportunity to escape. To hell with her promise, and to hell with Walt. If she could make a run for it, she would. All she needed was the chance to put space between her and Walt so she could bolt.

Unfortunately, the opportunity never came to fruition. As much as her legs were bouncing up and down in anticipation, she couldn't risk racing for the door, only to have him catch her. She already knew he was strong, so it was easy to assume he could probably run fast as well. And what if he really was good friends with the police chief? What if he killed her instead? She just couldn't take the chance.

After listening for an hour to several bar patrons trying their best at their renditions of *New York, New York* and Adele's *Hello,* Walt said it was time to leave.

He placed one hand on her elbow to guide her towards the door.

"Don't look so sad, Little Rose. You were a very good girl. Maybe we can do this again sometime."

Deshawna tried not to show her panic. This could be her only chance to get away, and she didn't want to blow it, but he had a firm grasp on her arm, and the bar was too crowded to allow her to make a run for it. With him literally attached to her, he could catch her easily before she'd gotten more than two steps away. The best she could hope for would be to ask Walt if they could do it again.

The opportunity came two weeks later. Deshawna had been asking Walt if they could go back to the bar. She reminded him how well-behaved she'd been at the bar the first time and promised again that she'd behave. Or maybe they could go to church, she suggested. She told him she loved going to church and that she was an active member of the AME Zion church. Could they go to the store together, she asked? She told him endless stories of shopping at the mall with her little sister. She was relentless in her pleading.

Finally, with a chuckle, Walt agreed. "I have to run a couple errands today. Would you like to go with me?"

"Oh, my God, yes! Yes, I would love to go!" Deshawna jumped up from the mattress and headed towards the ladder.

"Slow down, Little Rose. You need to put on the clothes you wore to the bar. Get dressed, and I'll be back in a few minutes." Walt climbed up the ladder, leaving Deshawna to get changed from the dirty T-shirt and sweatpants she wore every single day into the jeans and sweatshirt she had worn on their first outing. Deshawna could tell from the smell of the clothes that Walt had brought back freshly laundered clothes to her, while her everyday clothes, which she had worn since he'd abducted her, remained filthy and unwashed. She took a moment to press the sweatshirt to her nose and inhaled deeply. The smell of freshly laundered clothes was awesome.

A few minutes later, Walt returned to the bunker. Again, he blindfolded his captive before he led her out of the house and into the car. Little did he know, Deshawna had already devised a plan to gain her freedom. The blindfold was an inconsequential part in her plan.

Chapter Nineteen

With Deshawna blindfolded in the seat next to him, Walt drove directly to the bottle return center, only a few miles from his house. Last time, when he had brought Deshawna to the karaoke bar, he had driven in a zig-zag pattern, just in case she was keeping track of the twists and turns from his house. This time, she noticed there was no stop and go, no twists and turns to speak of; he apparently drove directly to the store. What he didn't realize was that Deshawna was, in fact, paying attention to the few turns and the amount of time it took to get to their destination, as best as she could figure without being able to look at a clock.

Walt removed the blindfold just before pulling into the parking lot. Deshawna noted the sign on the door—Second Chance Bottle Return. Walt parked the car close to the door. "Come on. I need your help to bring in some bottles and cans."

After opening the passenger door from the outside to let her out, Walt waited to make sure she walked with him to the back of the car. He opened the trunk. Deshawna's eyes were spinning back and forth as she took in as many landmarks as she could. She was trying to be inconspicuous. She kept her head level and only moved her eyes. If Walt knew she was trying to find out where they were, he might not let her out again.

The parking lot of the bottle return was nearly empty, but a Middle Eastern market next door looked busy. More cars were in their parking lot than in the lot of the bottle exchange. Maybe she could run to the market.

"Hey, I need your help here." Walt tapped her on the shoulder as he was speaking to her. She looked at him and saw the scrutinizing look in his eyes. If she ran now, he would be on her immediately. She had to wait until he became distracted.

He pulled a large garbage bag of bottles from the trunk and thrust it in her direction. She stepped back, caught off guard by the large bag he pushed at her.

She had no choice but to take it from him while he grabbed another large bag.

Deshawna inspected Walt's car. It looked old. It was tan, but other than that, she couldn't tell what make or model it was. To her, it was just a really old tan car. Damn! She wanted to know what kind of car he was driving.

As they walked into the building, she noted a phone hanging on the wall behind the cash register. She followed Walt to the far end of the room, where he opened his bag and started emptying the cans and bottles onto a dirty metal counter. Her pulse quickened as she formulated a plan. It was now or never.

"Hey, I have an idea," she said quietly. Her eyes bounced between Walt and the man behind the counter, whose attention was focused on counting the beverage containers. "There's a phone right there. Can I call the Catholic church to find out what time bingo starts? Maybe we could go sometime. I went a couple times with my mom and my aunt, and we had a blast. That would be fun, right?" She gave him her best smile and widened her eyes. She was hoping she looked excited about the idea and not freakish.

Walt's eyes spun as he looked from the phone to the man counting the bottles to Deshawna and back again, as if weighing her request, and whether or not he should allow her to be that far from him. It was only about ten feet away.

"Yeah, okay, but make it quick." He then lowered his voice. "And remember our deal." He looked at the clerk behind the counter, but he was too busy counting the bottles to pay attention to his customer's conversation.

Walt quietly said to her, "I'll be watching."

"No problem. I'll be quick. Bingo will be fun, right?" She spun towards the phone, resisting the urge to run from him. She had a better, safer idea.

Deshawna dialed the number she knew by heart. It was her older sister Naomi's cell phone. Naomi picked up on the second ring. Deshawna had counted on that, which is why she called her. Naomi's phone was never too far away from her.

"Naomi, it's me, Deshawna. Listen to..." Deshawna spoke in a whisper.

"Dee! Where the hell have you been? Oh, my God! Where are you?" Naomi was shrieking into the phone.

"Naomi, shut up and listen to me for a minute. I don't have much time. I was kidnapped by some guy named Walt and kept in a bunker..."

"You can't be serious," interrupted Naomi.

"Will you shut the hell up? Listen to me. I'm very serious, and I haven't got much time. We're at the Second Chance Bottle Return. I don't know where it is, but we're here now." There was a momentary pause before DeShawna began speaking louder. Walt was behind her. "Oh, yes, um. Seven o'clock. Thank you, yes. We'll be there. Thank you." Deshawna hung up the phone.

"Good news," she said, brightly. "Bingo starts at seven. Can we go? It would be a lot of fun, don't you think?" She realized she was rambling, but she was anxious. She wasn't sure how much he had heard.

Without a word, Walt walked back to the clerk, who was still busy counting cans.

Naomi was beside herself with excitement. Deshawna was alive! Holy crap! But what the hell was she saying before she hung up? Naomi paced back and forth, trying to decide what to do next. She had to find her sister, but how? She needed to find out where this bottle return place was. But what was it called? She'd been too shocked to absorb that information. Naomi hit the redial button on her cell. A male voice greeted her on the other end.

"Hello, Second Chance Bottle Return. Can I help you?"

"Yes, um, my sister just called me from this phone. Is she there?"

"No, they just left," the clerk said.

"Shit. Listen. My sister just called me from there. She's been missing for over six months." Naomi's heart was pounding in her chest so hard she thought the man on the other end of the phone could probably hear it. "When she called me, she said a guy named Walt had kidnapped her. We need to find them. Do you know where they are?"

"Uh, no. Not really. But on the way out, Walt said something about going to the pet store for bird seed. There's a pet store about two blocks from here. Maybe they went there."

"Okay. I need you to call 9-1-1 and give them that information. It would be better if you did it because I don't know where you're located. I don't know your address. I'm going to hang up, but I want you to call 9-1-1 right now, okay? Will you do that, please?"

"Yeah, sure. I'll call." The clerk hung up the phone, but instead of calling the police, the clerk called his boss, who happened to be a manager at the same pet store he suspected Walt and the young girl may have gone to.

The clerk called his boss's cell phone, but it went to voicemail. He disconnected the call without leaving a message. He waited a moment and tried again. This time, his boss picked up.

"Hey, Chuck. This is Mickey. I just got a strange call from some chick who said

Walt Pyke was here at the bottle exchange with a girl he'd supposedly kidnapped, and the girl was this chick's sister. I heard Walt say they were going to the pet store for bird seed. Are they there?"

"Whoa, slow down. Walt and some girl were just here, but they bought the seed and left. You said he kidnapped the girl he was with? What are you talking about?"

"That's what this chick said. All I know is the girl that was with Walt used the phone while Walt was turning in his usual shitload of returnables. Then the chick who called here said the girl who was with Walt called her from here and that she was the girl's sister, and Walt had kidnapped her about six months ago. The sister wanted me to call 9-1-1."

"Damn. I'll call the police right now. I always knew that guy was weird." The pet store manager disconnected the phone call and dialed 9-1-1.

CHAPTER TWENTY

Sergeant Steve "Mac" MacIntosh had been enjoying his day off. He'd spent the morning with his son, Austin, and Alayna, his ex-wife, planting spring flowers at the house he had previously shared with them. After a long morning of gardening, followed by lunch consisting of hamburgers on the grill, macaroni salad and Alayna's fabulous chocolate cake, he had just gotten home to his own apartment, only a few minutes' drive away.

After a refreshing shower, Mac was watching a baseball game on the television when his cell phone rang. The caller ID showed it was someone from the police department calling.

With a groan, he picked up the phone. "Steve MacIntosh."

"Hey, Sarge. This is Heidi. We have a call that I think you're going to want to know about."

With a sigh, Mac asked, "What's up?"

"A young girl called her sister from a bottle return place and told the sister she'd been kidnapped by some guy named Walt and has been held in a bunker for several months. According to the store manager at the bottle return, Walt and the girl are heading to a pet store on Route 290. We've got units en route to the pet store right now, so I thought you'd want to know."

Mac lifted his feet from the coffee table in front of him and bolted upright. He was silent for a few moments as he absorbed the news.

"Sarge, are you still there?" Heidi asked.

"Yeah, I'm here. I'm on my way." Mac disconnected the call. He didn't even bother to change out of his jeans and Baltimore Orioles T-shirt, merely grabbing his car keys and heading out the door. A few minutes later, he'd made record time getting to Route 290.

Mac pulled into the parking lot just as two officers were walking out of the pet store. He dispensed with the formalities of saying hello and got right to the point. "Did you find them?"

One of the officers shook her head. "No, but the manager identified the male as Walter Pyke and said he lives on Battle Creek Road. The manager got Pyke's address from the check he just wrote. We're heading there now."

Mac spun on his heels and jumped in his car. He followed the marked police car out of the parking lot with tires squealing. To Mac, the ear-piercing noise reminded him of a cat with its tail caught under the rungs of a rocking chair, but this time, he barely heard it. His concentration was on finding Walter Pyke and the girl.

Mac called Heidi and Coop, who were only minutes behind, on the portable radio. "We missed Walt and the young girl at the pet store, but the store manager said this Walt guy lives on Battle Creek Road. We're headed there now."

Mac turned his portable radio to the 9-1-1 channel and alerted the dispatcher to his change of location. "I want all available units to respond to that address. No lights or sirens. Have them wait for me before we make entry into the home. I'd like an ambulance to respond as a precaution as well."

The officers arriving ahead of Mac pulled to the side of the road and parked adjacent to a large hedgerow that blocked the view of the house. Mac barely stopped before throwing the gear shift into park. As he exited his car, Mac's investigator skills kicked in as he took in the sight, making mental notes of the scenario. Tall arborvitae trees almost completely surrounded the house on the outskirts of the property. The only break between them was for the driveway, making the house well-concealed from the neighbors and the traffic on Battle Creek Road. Mac noticed several rose gardens on the three sides of the house that he could see, with one garden standing independently in the middle of a side yard. He wondered if Walt had planted that one on top of the bunker. The thought sent chills down his spine.

Parked in the driveway in front of the ranch house was a tan Dodge Daytona. The vehicle was just as Emily Tuttle had described during her statement from the previous year. Mac's heart began to race. His palms grew sweaty. After all these years, Mac knew this had to be the kidnapper. Finally!

But Mac would have to find out why it didn't show up on the Department of Motor Vehicles search that Heidi had done. For now, he pushed that thought to the back of his mind.

Mac heard a couple more cars pull in behind him. He looked over his shoulder and saw Heidi and Coop exiting one of the cars. A few more uniformed officers arrived as well.

"I haven't seen anyone moving around since we got here," Mac said, his voice just above a whisper, "but I'm hoping Walt and his victim are inside. We need to be careful—I don't want that girl getting hurt."

Mac quickly took charge of planning the rescue by directing one of the officers to make entry through the front door using a battering ram. He asked some of the officers to surround the home on all four sides, just in case Pyke tried to get away. He then directed the remaining officers to follow him inside the home. Once inside, they would split up and search the rooms.

With guns drawn, the police officers quickly walked single file towards the house. As they passed the tan Dodge, Mac flattened his palm on the hood.

The metal was still very warm, which meant it had been driven recently.

The first group of officers branched off, with some weaving around the left side of the house, while others went to the right to surround the outside of the home. Mac approached the front door and yelled, "Police!" He took a step back while the cop with the battering ram let it fly, shattering the doorknob and lock with one swing of the heavy metal. Splinters of wood went flying as the door slammed inward. A flurry of cops entered the home and snaked their way into each room, searching for Walt and his victim.

Mac saw an older man wearing khakis and oversized glasses enter the kitchen from an open door on the opposite side of the room. The officers raised their guns and began yelling at once. "Stop, police!" "Put your hands up!" "Get on the ground!"

The man froze in his tracks, clearly stunned. He fell to his knees, his head swiveling from left to right as he looked at the cops surrounding him. One of the officers lowered the man face-first onto the floor and pulled his hands behind his back. The man winced as handcuffs were placed around his wrists. The cop then helped him into a sitting position on the floor.

Mac stepped forward. "What's your name?"

"What's going on?"

"Sir, what's your name?" Mac said again.

"Walter Pyke. What's going on?"

"You had a girl with you. Where is she?"

Mac watched as the color drained from Walter's face. "What girl? I don't have a girl with me. Can't you see that?"

Mac pointed at Walt. "Watch him," he said to one of the officers. "The rest of you come with me." Mac headed towards the door Walter had just come through.

Seeing the trail of open doors, they worked their way through the empty garage and down a set of stairs into the basement.

"Holy crap," Mac said. "Look at all these shelves. Let's split up and search for the girl."

Within a few moments, Coop called out. "Over here!"

Mac wound his way between the shelves until he found his partner standing in front of an empty metal shelving unit. Devoid of any bottles or cans, it seemed out of place among the other shelves that were packed full. One side of the unit was pulled a few inches away from the wall, as if it were a door that hadn't closed all the way.

Coop pulled it the rest of the way from the wall, the metal shelf giving an obnoxious screech as it scraped across the concrete floor. Once opened, another partly open door was exposed, and beyond that, a small, open area, about the size of a small closet. They rushed in, only to find another door that had also been left open a few inches. They worked their way through the doors until they reached what looked like a tunnel.

Heidi began calling out. "Hello! Hello? Is anyone there?"

After several seconds, a faint voice could be heard. "Who's there?"

Heidi was the first one to enter the tunnel, crawling head-first towards the voice she instinctively knew would belong to the young girl. Coop used the flashlight on his cell phone to light as much of the tunnel as he could. When Heidi got to the end, she looked through the opening. A girl was standing in the center of a small room, her hands covering her mouth.

"It's okay. I'm an investigator with the police department," Heidi said. "My name is Heidi, and you're safe now." She twisted and turned until she could reach the step ladder, feet first. She climbed down into the bunker.

The girl, who looked to be about fourteen or fifteen, backed up further into the bunker.

"It's okay. I'm not going to hurt you," Heidi said.

Coop had followed Heidi through the tunnel and had stopped at the entrance to the bunker. He was carefully watching the interaction between Heidi and the young woman before he climbed down.

"Are you going to give me to the police chief?" the young woman asked, her voice barely above a whisper. The fear in her eyes was evident.

"What? No, we're not here to give you to anyone. We're here to take you home. It's okay. No one is going to hurt you." Heidi held her hands in front of her, palms outward, in a show that everything will be okay.

Suddenly, DeShawna launched herself into Heidi's arms and buried her face in the investigator's shoulder. Uncontrollable sobs wracked her body as Heidi gently rubbed her back and murmured shushing noises. "It's okay. Everything will be okay. Shh. You're safe now."

Coop and Mac lowered themselves into the bunker, the much-larger men having a more difficult time than Heidi. They looked around, in case there were more than one girl in the bunker.

"What's your name?" said Heidi.

"My name is DeShawna Washington. Can I go home now?"

"Absolutely. Let's get you outside, okay?"

DeShawna vigorously nodded her head in agreement as she swiped at the tears from her cheeks.

"Where's Walt?" DeShawna asked.

"He's in custody."

A slight smile formed on DeShawna's lips.

Heidi led the way through the tunnel. Once they were outside, Heidi brought DeShawna to the paramedics at the waiting ambulance.

Mac and Coop took a few minutes to look around the bunker before they left. It was clearly the same bunker that Gabriella, Yen and Emily had described.

Once outside, Mac and Coop went to check on DeShawna and found her sitting on the edge of the gurney in the ambulance. Both hands gripped a blanket tightly around her shoulders. She held her head back with her eyes closed. It looked to Mac as if she was praying to the ceiling of the ambulance. A paramedic sat in front of her, writing something on a clipboard.

Mac approached Heidi, who was standing near the back of the ambulance. "How is she?" Mac asked quietly, tossing his head towards their victim.

"She's doing okay, all things considered," Heidi said. "I talked to her for a bit, but I didn't want to press her too hard. She's pretty traumatized, although that's totally understandable. She's only sixteen. She said that Walt, or should I say the suspect, kidnapped her about six, almost seven months ago. The suspect has been sexually abusing her every day for that entire time. It's disgusting. She's just a kid." Heidi was glaring at the police car that held Walt as if her eyes could send a message of revolt to their perp.

"The rest of the team has been in the main part of the house to make sure there are no other victims but didn't find anyone," Mac said. "Pyke had denied that DeShawna was there, let alone any others, so it's better to be safe than sorry. I've radioed Sgt. Marco DeLuca back at the station and asked him to get a search warrant. He should be here soon."

They watched in silence as the ambulance pulled onto the roadway and sped off towards the hospital with their young patient, the flashing lights reflecting off the legion of police vehicles now gathered in the driveway and on the road.

"Heidi," Mac said, "I'd like you to go to the hospital to be ready to interview the victim. After what she's been through, she might feel more comfortable talking with a female officer."

"You got it, Mac. I'll head over there now so I'll be on hand about the time she arrives. Once she's cleared by the medical team, I'll see what she has to say." Heidi turned on her heel and headed towards her car.

Just then, Marco walked up to Mac and Coop with a folded paper in his hand. "I've got the search warrant, Mac." He waved it in the air as if it were a blue ribbon at the county fair.

"Excellent. Thank you, Marco. Coop, why don't you and I go check out this bunker where the girls have been held and get a closer look. And before you ask, yes, I said girls, plural. This has got to be our guy."

As Mac and Coop walked through the front door of Walt's house, Mac looked around at what would normally be considered a living room with a sofa, an old box-style television on a small, blonde-colored stand, and a couple matching end tables. Leaning stacks of magazines and papers covered the end tables and even the top of the television. More piles littered the floor, some leaning on each other so they wouldn't topple over. Only the seat of a recliner was free from the clutter.

What Mac didn't know was that the cleaning and sorting Yen had done six years before had been in vain. The house was again a hoarder's nightmare.

In their search for the victim when they first entered the home, they had not looked closely at the condition of their surroundings. Now they could take their time, look at the detritus throughout the house, and get a general picture of who their suspect really was.

Coop led the way as they walked down a hallway and into the kitchen. Mac stopped to look at the mess on the counters. He'd never seen so many takeout containers in his life! They appeared clean, but there must have been over a hundred of them, stacked one inside the other, and covering every available inch of counter space. Mac just shook his head.

They went down the stairs, Coop still in the lead. Mac's chin dropped as he looked over the hundreds—no, thousands—of bottles and cans lining the dozens of shelving units that crowded the basement floor.

"What the hell?" was all Mac could say as he tried to absorb the immensity of what he was gazing at.

"Yeah, right? This guy has some kind of bottle fetish. Most of them are all different, too. They look like they're from all over the world," said Coop. "Pretty crazy, huh?"

"You're not kidding," Mac said, still looking over the collection of beverage containers. "I don't know if this guy should be considered a hoarder or a collector."

"Maybe both," said Coop with a chuckle. "I hate to say this, but getting into the bunker is almost ingenious, although I don't want to give the pervert that much credit." He stopped in front of the empty metal shelving unit, oddly out of place from the others that were filled to overflowing with bottles and cans. "This is the shelving unit you have to pull away from the wall to expose the hidden door behind it." Coop closed and then opened the faux door to demonstrate, the squeak sending chills up Mac's spine.

"Good lord, that's like nails on a chalkboard!" Mac shook at the sound.

"Sorry, boss," Coop tried unsuccessfully to hide his grin as he watched his boss shiver.

"We need the evidence technician to take photos of the entire house. Has he been down here yet?" Mac asked.

"Patrick O'Malley is here, and he's doing the ET work. I think right now he's checking out the rooms upstairs. I can get him down here if you want."

"Yeah, let's have him come down and take photos as we go, before we disturb anything."

Coop called Patrick on the hand-held radio, but he was already on his way into the basement. He was taking photographs throughout the house, but unlike the investigators, Patrick was a uniformed officer and also wore a body camera that would take a video as they made their way into the bunker. The photos and videos were an important part of any investigation, and O'Malley was among the best evidence technicians on the force.

Once they had moved the shelf, they faced the door that was hidden behind it. Mac and O'Malley followed Coop into the tight four foot by four foot space. Reaching up, O'Malley pulled the string to turn on the overhead light bulb. They stood looking at the other door on the opposite wall. An open padlock hung from the door frame.

"With the amount of deterrents this guy has to protect the bunker, there's no way anyone else would have ever discovered it," Mac said. "The scary part is that if something ever happened to Walter while he had a victim in here, no one would have ever known. She could have died down there."

"That's very true. Thank God that didn't happen, but it makes you wonder if anyone else knew about the bunker," Coop said. "Could he have told someone, just in case?"

"That's a good question," Mac said. "It's hard to say how a mind like that works. He may have wanted to keep the girls to himself, but you would think someone in the family would have seen him bringing food to the basement. Who else lives here? Does anyone know?"

"I don't know. I haven't talked to the guy, but that's a good question."

Coop reached for the handle to open the second door. It wouldn't stay open, so O'Malley went back into the basement and found something heavy to use as a doorstop. He came back with a large ceramic jug to prop the door open.

"Looks like he has a padlock on the front of both doors, but there's also a latch on the back of the doors." O'Malley observed, pointing to the hasp on the outer edge of the door frame they had just come through. He craned his neck to see the other part of the hasp on the back of the door. "I'm thinking he might have thrown the lock from the front of the door to the back when he was inside the bunker with the girls."

"That would make sense. He probably figured that way, they wouldn't be able to overpower him and escape when he was with them," Mac agreed. "And with a combination lock on this door, there's no way the victim could have gotten out unless he gave her the combination. It's not like she could pick his pockets for the keys. That would work on the other lock but not this one."

"Okay, let's take another look at this bunker," Mac said. "O'Malley, just so you know, we're going to have better luck crawling through the tunnel backwards."

"Are you serious?" O'Malley asked, his eyes wide. "Backwards?"

"Yep. There's a stepladder at the far end we'll have to climb down and there's not much room for us to turn around at the end of the tunnel. Coop, do you have your flashlight with you?"

"My cell phone. That's it," Coop said.

"That's fine. It worked for Heidi when she went through the tunnel," Mac said.

"Okay. After you, partner," said Coop.

"Just give me a bit of space before you follow. I don't feel like getting smacked in the head by your size twelves," joked Mac. With Mac in the lead, Coop and O'Malley backed into the tunnel, crawling on their hands and knees.

They all understood that the situation they were investigating was not a laughing matter. Far from it. But the levity helped them cope, if only for a moment, with the horrific crimes against young women that took place in the bunker.

At the end of the tunnel, the men climbed down the stepladder and into the bunker. The air was ripe with the smell of dampness, mold, urine, feces, and body odor. They looked at the makeshift toilet, the tub, and the garden hose hanging over the tub without uttering a word.

Mac looked at the graffiti on the walls and recognized the words Gabrielle Reyes said she'd written. His instincts were right. Deshawna was not the first victim to be held within these concrete walls and the graffiti proved it. One man had been kidnapping women and holding them in a bunker, and they had finally found him.

Walking into the pseudo-bedroom next, Mac stared at the thin, dirty mattress lying on the floor. He saw no sheets, only a threadbare blanket that had seen much better days. The chains that ended in handcuffs were on the floor next to the filthy mattress. His stomach clenched as he tried not to think of the disgusting criminal acts that must have taken place in this spot. He closed his eyes and drew a deep breath through his mouth, trying to minimize the odor.

When Mac opened his eyes, he focused on the monthly calendar pinned to the wall. A small, red crayon hung from the push pin with a bit of string. On every day of that month, there was an initial S written with the red crayon. Every two or three days—sometimes more—there was also a B or T. The last entry was from a day before where a red S was written within the one-inch-square box.

"Phew. This blows my mind. I mean, I know what he did to those women. I was horrified when I took their statements, but visiting this bunker helps me grasp the magnitude of what he did to them. What a horrible, evil place this is.

Someday, when it's all over and done, and this asshole is in prison for life, I hope it's blown apart with dynamite."

Coop and O'Malley could only nod in agreement. "I'd love to be the one to light the fuse," Coop said with a scowl on his face.

CHAPTER TWENTY-ONE

Mac drove the long way around to get back to the police department. He needed the extra few minutes to decompress after seeing the bunker. Women had endured both physical and mental abuse in that chamber of horrors and he could not—did not—want to imagine any of it. What kind of sicko were they dealing with? Had there been other women they didn't know about yet? Women who hadn't come forward? The thought made him sick to his stomach. There were gaps in the timeline as they knew it, so it was entirely possible.

Had anyone died there? That might account for the gaps. Mac would do his best to find the answers. He owed it to the victims.

As Mac approached the door to the police department, he took a deep, cleansing breath to suppress the anger that was building inside him. He needed to interview the suspect, but he knew it would take as much strength as he could muster to talk civilly to this Walter Pyke character.

Mac walked into the CID office to find Coop and Heidi already there and waiting for him. O'Malley had stayed behind to process the bunker for evidence. He would photograph each item in the bunker, then store the smaller items in their own clear plastic bags, in case they were required later at trial.

They planned to bring back the mattress and test it for DNA, leaving the larger items like the toilet and the tub, behind. Removing those items would mean enlarging the tunnel, but that would render the tunnel useless as evidence. If necessary, they would tackle that problem down the road.

How Pyke even got those items in the bunker remained a mystery to Mac. He would have to add that question to his growing list of questions he'd have to ask their suspect.

After a uniformed officer transported him to the department, they had brought Walt into the interview room while Coop watched him through the surveillance camera until Mac arrived. The investigators would talk to their suspect together.

"Are you ready for this, Mac? You look kind of pissed off," asked Coop.

"I'm pissed, for sure, but I'm more disgusted. What this guy did to women is reprehensible." Mac shook his head in disbelief. "Has Walt been Mirandized yet?"

"Yes," Coop said. "The officer that transported him here read him his rights before he was brought to the PD."

"Okay. As long as it's on body camera, we're good. I'm going to have him sign for it on paper, also, just to be sure. The last thing we need is to have this guy get off on a technicality if the body cam video got lost or something."

"Sarge," Heidi said, "do you mind if I go into the interview with you and observe? I hate to put it this way, but it might be a good learning tool."

"Sure, you can definitely sit in on the interview with us. That's a good idea. Let me grab a cup of coffee first, though." Mac took his time at the coffee machine before announcing to the investigators they might as well get started.

Heidi grabbed a chair from the conference room and brought it into the interview room. The others had already taken their seats. The room was rather tight with four people and a small table occupying the space. Walt shifted in his seat as the three investigators crowded the room, his eyes lingering on Heidi. Mac wasn't sure if Walt was staring at Heidi because he liked the way she looked or because he resented having a woman of authority present. Either way, Mac wasn't concerned with his suspect's feelings or comfort level.

As he took a seat, Mac made the introductions. "Mr. Pyke, I'm Sergeant MacIntosh and this is Investigator Cooper and Investigator Thompson."

Walt muttered a simple hello.

"I understand an officer has informed you of your Miranda rights before bringing you here to the police department. However, I have a form right here that also lists your Miranda rights, and I'd like you to initial after each one as I read them to you. This is for our records."

Mac placed the form in front of Walt and read his rights to him as Walt initialed on each respective line. Walt was still wearing the handcuffs, although they were now cinched in front of him, making it cumbersome to write on the table.

"So, you understand why you're here, correct?" asked Mac.

"I guess so, kind of," Walt said. "I'm not under arrest, am I?"

The investigators just looked at each other. "Yes, you are under arrest," Mac said. "You're being charged with four counts of kidnapping, four counts of rape, and two counts of sexual misconduct against a child. As the investigation progresses, we may add more charges as well."

"Why all those charges?" whined Walt. "I don't understand."

"Well, let me enlighten you," Coop said with a smirk. "We got a call earlier today about a young lady who said you kidnapped her about six months ago. You kept her in an underground bunker against her will and raped her on a daily basis. Does that ring a bell?"

"I didn't kidnap anyone!" argued Walt.

Mac wrote a quick note in his notebook that it was the kidnapping accusation Walt objected to, but he hadn't denied the rapes.

"What do you call it when you grab women off the street, hold them captive, and then don't let them leave?" Heidi interjected.

"Yes, I made them stay in the bunker, but I did it for health reasons. If I let them out and they had sex with someone else, I could get a sexually transmitted disease. This way, we could have sex, and I wouldn't catch anything."

The room was silent as Mac, Coop, and Heidi tried to make sense of his logic. Finally, Mac spoke. "Why did you do this? Why did you kidnap these women? And yes, it is kidnapping, regardless of what you might think. Taking someone against their will and not letting them leave is a kidnapping. So, why did you do it?"

"My wife got cancer in 2006. It was a female type of cancer, so she couldn't have sex anymore. But a man has certain urges, you know what I mean? So, these women would stay with me, and we would have sex. But I took care of them. I gave them food. They would take a bath and brush their teeth. They had a radio, and I even brought them magazines. All they had to do was have sex. Pretty easy, right?" Walt looked between Mac and Coop and back again, his eyebrows raised as if he was waiting for them to agree, or at least understand what he was saying. He avoided looking at Heidi.

Mac was biting the inside of his lip so he didn't say anything that he shouldn't. Coop was tapping his fingers on the table in a quick, steady beat, and Heidi sat with her mouth slightly open, staring at the suspect in disbelief. Walt's line of thinking was definitely twisted. However, it did not escape the investigators that he had also just confessed to having more than one victim.

"When you say, 'these women,' exactly how many are we talking about?" Coop asked.

Walt realized his mistake and tried to cover it up. "I don't know. Just one or two is all."

"Oh, come on, Walt. A man like you with those kinds of urges? I'll bet you've had lots of women in that bomb shelter of yours," Coop suggested. "You take care of them and all you ask is that they show you a little appreciation, right?"

Over time, Coop and Mac had become very adept at playing the good cop/bad cop routine. Sometimes Mac would be the "good" cop, while at other times, they would switch, and Coop would play the "good" cop. This time, it was Coop.

"Yeah, that's right. Just a little appreciation. That's all I asked," Walt said, as he gave Coop a sly smile. "You know what I mean by that, right?"

"Yeah, I know what you mean," Coop said. "It sounds like they had a pretty good life, living in that bunker of yours. From what you're saying, they lived rent free, you gave them food, their own bed and they didn't even have to stand in line for the bathroom. It was all theirs with no waiting."

"That's it. They were lucky I took such good care of them," Walt said.

"So, c'mon, Walt. Tell me how many women lived in the bunker. How many were lucky enough?"

"Well, um, like I said, only a couple of women. That's all."

"That's not true, Walter," Mac said. The muscles in his jaw tightened as he clenched and unclenched his teeth. "We know you had multiple women in the bunker. Be honest with us. We want to know how many you've had in there."

"Like I said, just one or two. That's it," Walt stammered.

"The problem is, Walt, we know you kidnapped more than one or two women. You see, we've had more than one or two women come to us and report that they had been held in an underground bunker by a guy named Walt. These women described you and the bunker to a 'T.'"

"What I'd like to know," continued Mac, "is how did you get them to come with you? How did you convince them to be your sex slaves?"

"I don't like the way you said that. You make it sound like I'm some kind of pervert. Some kind of monster."

Coop said, "How did you do it, Walt? How did you get them to go with you? They weren't prostitutes looking for their next customer. What did you say to them to get them to get in the car with you?" He was using a softer tone to try to get Walt to give up the details. Details they already knew but were looking for confirmation of.

Walt hesitated. He seemed to be thinking a bit before he spoke up. "I offered them rides, and they accepted is all."

"What exactly did you say to them?" Coop pressed.

"I asked if they wanted a ride, and if they said yes, then I offered to drive them home. What they didn't realize is that I meant my home not theirs. Eventually, after they'd stayed with me for a bit, I let them go so they could go back to their homes, so I didn't exactly break my promise. It just took longer than they expected, is all." Walt smiled at his cleverness.

"What kind of car do you have?" Mac wanted to know why the search in the Department of Motor Vehicles database for the 1984 Dodge Daytona hadn't produced a match, and yet, they had seen a car matching that description in front of the house.

"I have two different cars, but I always drove the old Dodge Daytona when I was out bottle hunting or women hunting. A lot of times, if I'm running errands, I have a Chevy Impala that I use."

"What year is the Dodge?" Mac asked.

"It's a 1985 Dodge Daytona." Mac and Coop looked at each other. That would explain why it didn't appear in their search. Emily Tuttle was certain it was a 1984 model and Mac wondered if that may have been the only year Heidi had searched for. He would have to ask her after the interrogation with Walt but judging by the stricken look he saw on her face, he would say she hadn't thought to run more than the one year she was asked to run.

"Is it registered in Maryland?" Mac asked.

"Well, yes and no. It used to be, but I haven't renewed the registration in a few years."

Mac felt better about that, knowing that even if Heidi had searched for a 1985 Dodge Daytona, the information on Walter's vehicle still wouldn't have popped up. He glanced at Heidi, and the look of relief on her face let him know that she had also realized that.

"Who else lives with you in the house?" Mac was thinking of the conversation at the bunker between Coop and himself.

"No one. I live alone, ever since my wife died," Walt said.

"How did you get these women to crawl through the tunnel into the bunker?" Coop asked.

Walt shrugged his shoulders. "I just asked them to do it, and they did."

"Did you threaten them at all? Did you physically force them into your house, the tunnel, or the bunker?"

"I don't remember." Walt was obviously lying.

"Once you got these women into the bunker, what did you do?" Coop asked.

Walt looked at Heidi, as if he was hesitant to say.

"It's okay, Walt. Just pretend I'm not even here," she said.

"Well, we usually had sex first, then I showed them around. You know, showed them where they would sleep, take a bath, and use the toilet."

"Did they have sex willingly?" asked Mac.

"Not at first, but eventually they did."

"Did you force yourself on them, Walt? When they weren't willing, I mean?"

"Well, sure. I had to show them who's the boss." Walt turned his handcuffed hands palm up, as if it was an obvious answer. "Besides, it costs money to feed them, so they had to earn their keep."

"Why did you make them write those initials on the calendar? The S, B, and T?" Coop asked.

"I like to be organized. I try to keep track of things, and I thought it was important to keep track of when they brushed their teeth, took a bath, or when we had sex. I enjoy having sex every day; it keeps me young and healthy. So, when they put the B and T on the calendar, it showed I was taking care of them. That was my thanks to them for the sex."

"Why the red crayon? Did that signify something?" Mac asked.

"Not really. I wasn't going to give them a pen or pencil because I watched a movie one time where a guy stabbed another guy in the eye with a pencil. I heard that's why they're not allowed in prisons, either. I don't want to get stabbed, so I gave them the crayon."

Mac wanted to keep Walt talking for as long as possible. "Let's talk about Gabrielle Reyes. Was she your first captive?"

"No, she wasn't," Walt said.

Mac quickly offered an almost indiscernible sideways glance at Coop. Gabrielle had been the first one to report her kidnapping to the police, but Walt had just admitted she was not his first. That confirmed their suspicions that there were other women who hadn't come forward.

"How many came before Gabrielle?" Coop asked.

"Um, I don't remember. That was a long time ago." Walt started shifting in his seat, uncomfortable with this line of questioning. Beads of sweat had appeared on Walt's forehead. "Can I have some water or coffee or something?"

Heidi stood up. "I'll get it." She returned a moment later with a paper cup of water.

"So, Walt, tell us about Gabrielle." Mac wanted to continue pressing Walt for the details.

"What's to tell? She was with me for a while, then I drove her home."

"Did you know how old she was when you took her?" Mac asked.

"First of all, I didn't take her. She came with me willingly. But to answer your question, no. I didn't know how old she was. It turned out she looked older than she really was."

"Do you like them young, Walt?" Mac asked.

"I don't care about age. It's not their face I'm interested in." Walt chuckled at his own joke.

Mac was working hard to control his emotions. He took a breath before he continued. "Why did you refer to the women as 'Little Flower' or 'Little Rose'?"

"That was a term of endearment. You see, I enjoy growing roses in my gardens around the house. I like to nurture the rose bushes until they develop into beautiful creations. I looked at these women the same way. I would teach them and nurture them until they became beautiful. If they learned to have great sex and performed well, I called them my Little Rose or my Precious Rose."

"And if they didn't?" asked Mac.

"Didn't what?" Walt asked.

"Didn't perform well? What would you do?"

"Nothing. I would continue teaching them until they learned how to do what was expected of them perfectly."

"Did you tell these women you belonged to a sex club, along with some powerful men? Men like the police chief, celebrities, and political figures?"

Walt had the decency to hang his head. After several seconds of silence, he finally admitted he had said that.

"And is that the truth? Do you really belong to a sex club?"

"No, there isn't any club. I made it up." Walt smiled at his wit.

"Why did you tell them that?"

"I didn't want them thinking they could run away. I figured if I could put some fear in them, they would stay put."

"Do you even *know* the chief of police?" Mac highly doubted that.

"No, I've never even met him, but the women didn't know that." Walt smiled, as if he appreciated his own cleverness.

"Where did you get the badge you showed to the women?" Coop asked.

"I found it years ago when I was looking for cans and bottles on the side of the road. I don't remember exactly what street it was on, but I saw it partly hidden under a bush, so I just grabbed it and kept it."

"Speaking of cans and bottles, why do you have so many in your basement? There has to be a few thousand down there," Coop asked.

"Actually, there are over ten thousand. I enjoy collecting things, especially bottles and cans. Some of them are quite beautiful, and they're all different. Especially the foreign ones."

"Some people would call that hoarding," Mac pointed out.

Walt gave Mac a dirty look. "It's not hoarding. It's collecting, and there's a difference. I only keep bottles and cans that I like, and if I have too many of the same bottle, I take the extras to the bottle and can exchange. I only keep two or three of each one. Do you mind if we take a break? I could use the bathroom."

Mac and Heidi returned to the CID office while Coop showed Walt to the prisoner's bathroom. Once Coop returned him to the interview room, they would watch Walt on the surveillance camera for a few minutes before resuming the interrogation. For now, they all needed a break to decompress.

CHAPTER TWENTY-TWO

Mac, Coop and Heidi discussed their opinions of the interview as they watched the security camera to see their suspect put his head down on the interview room table. If he was tired after a long day, he would get no sympathy from the investigators.

"The man's a dirtbag," said Heidi, her lips curled like she'd just eaten a bug. "He's repulsive. I wanted to trip him in the hallway and watch him fall on his face when you took him to the bathroom."

"He's a monster." Mac shook his head in disgust. "By his own admission, there have to be women he kidnapped that we don't know about. I think we need to get a press release out as soon as possible after he's arraigned. Maybe those women will come forward if they know they're not alone."

"There was something I was wondering about," Coop said. "The man admitted he enjoyed collecting things. Of the victims we know about, the first was Hispanic, the second Oriental, the third Caucasian, and the last was Black. I wonder if he collected his victims like he collected his bottles. They were all different."

"Do you think he would have done that? Been that organized?" Heidi asked, wide-eyed.

"It seems that way, doesn't it?" admitted Mac. "Let's ask him."

Mac, Coop, and Heidi returned to the interview room. Walter Pyke had put his head down on the table while he waited.

"Okay, Walt. We should be able to wrap this up in a bit, but we still have just a few more questions," said Mac. "So, before we took a break, we'd been talking about your can and bottle collection. We noticed that each of your victims was of a different nationality. They were all different, just like your bottles and cans. Did you do that on purpose? Did you collect these women based on their nationality?" Mac was careful not to divulge how many women they knew about. He hoped Walt would fill in the blanks.

Walt grinned, as if he was pleased with himself. "Yes, I did. My wife used to tell me I have OCD. Maybe that's true, I don't know. But I do like to have everything organized and in order."

"What nationalities do you like, Walt?" Coop said.

"Oh, it doesn't matter to me. I like them all."

"How many different nationalities have you collected so far?"

Walt hesitated. "Like I said already, just one or two."

"Some of the women said you had them in handcuffs chained to the wall, sometimes for hours at a time. Why did you do that? It's not like they could escape the dungeon." Mac asked.

"There's no way they could get out because I always locked the doors behind me, even when I was with them. I handcuffed them to the wall so they wouldn't be able to fight so much. It was difficult getting the job done if they kept squirming and fighting. Eventually, I took them off once they learned who was boss. Besides, it wasn't a big deal. Women wear bracelets all the time."

"Why didn't you wear a condom?" Heidi asked. She had remained quiet throughout the interview, but this question begged to be answered.

"I didn't need to. The doctor did a 'snip snip' on me several years ago. I don't like to use condoms, anyway. I prefer au naturale."

Heidi gave an audible groan and shook her head.

"Okay, I think that's enough for now," said Mac, as he stood up and gathered his notes. "Give us some time to type up the paperwork, then we'll bring you in front of the judge to be arraigned, and you'll probably go to jail from there."

"I'll be in jail for what, maybe two or three days?" asked Walt.

"That depends. The judge might set a bail amount, or she may remand you without bail. That's up to her. If she sets the bail amount and you're able to make bail, she will release you. If you can't make bail, you'll be held in jail until you go to trial or plead to the charges."

Walt was stunned. "Seriously? I figured I'd have to go to jail for a couple days and do some kind of community service. How long before I go to trial?"

"It could take several months."

"Several months? And then what? I won't go to prison in the end, will I?" Walt was beginning to panic.

"That's entirely possible. It will depend on what you plea to, or if you go to trial, what you're found guilty of. The judge will assign an attorney when you're arraigned, if you can't afford one. The attorney will talk to you about your options."

With that, Mac, Coop, and Heidi left the interview room and closed the door behind them. From the surveillance camera, they watched as Walt put his head in his hands.

"I'm going to draw up the paperwork so we can get him arraigned," Mac said. "In the meantime, I'll call Judge Johannsen to see if she's available to do the arraignment. I'm sure the district attorney is going to want to be heard on a bail recommendation, so I'll give DA Wozniak a call as well."

Mac first called Judge Evelyn Johannsen's chambers and spoke to her secretary. The judge would be working late and would be available to arraign their suspect. As it turned out, she had been the judge who had signed the search warrant earlier for Walt's house. The secretary said the judge was already expecting to do an arraignment.

Mac's next call was to District Attorney Dennis Wozniak's office.

The phone rang twice before the DA picked up his phone. "Hi, Mac. How are you?"

"Doing well, sir. Thank you. How are you?"

"I'm doing great. What's up?"

"Well, we have quite a case for you. For several years—almost ten, actually—a guy by the name of Walter Pyke has been kidnapping women and keeping them as sex slaves in an underground bomb shelter connected to his house. His latest victim was able to make a phone call that led to his arrest, so we're looking to get him arraigned in the next hour or so. I thought you might like to suggest a bail recommendation."

There was silence on the other end of the phone. Mac wondered momentarily if he'd lost the phone connection. "Holy shit," Wozniak finally said.

Mac was a bit surprised at the language. It was a rarity when the DA cussed.

"How long has he been keeping these women captive? Were they held together?"

"No, they were all held at different times, and he took only one at a time, but he held each one anywhere from a few months to more than two years. He confessed in the interview to holding only one or two women, but he wouldn't say anything specific about them, just that he's held a couple women in his bunker. Because of several complaints over the years, we know of four victims for sure, but we suspect he kidnapped at least one more, and there could be others."

"I will definitely be there for the arraignment. Can you fax over the paperwork to me?"

"I'm sending it as we speak."

"I'll see you in a while, Mac." The DA disconnected the call.

An hour later, Mac and Coop brought Walt in front of the judge to be arraigned. Coop handed the paperwork to the court clerk as they approached the bench. The judge quietly read the complaint information and the victim's affidavits. Mac and Coop watched Judge Johannsen as her eyebrows rose and her facial expression changed from passive to one of disbelief. A couple times, she lifted her eyes from the papers to glance at the defendant standing in front of her.

When she'd finished reading, she proceeded with the arraignment. "Mr. Pyke, you're being charged with four counts of kidnapping in the first degree, four counts of rape in the first degree, four counts of performing a criminal sex act by force in the first degree, two counts of sexual misconduct against a child and four counts of sexual abuse, first degree." She asked Walt if he had an attorney.

"No, I don't. Do I really need one?" Walt asked.

"I would highly recommend it," said Judge Johannsen. "If you can't afford one, I will appoint one for you."

"Yes, I'd appreciate it if you would appoint one, Judge."

At that point, Judge Johannsen called the day's public defender, Declan Murphy, to the bench. She handed him a duplicate copy of the paperwork that Mac had provided to the court.

"How does your client plead, Counselor?"

As he glanced at the complaint information, Murphy said hesitantly, "Um, I'd like to enter a not guilty plea on behalf of my client, Your Honor." He never took his eyes off the papers he was reading.

"So noted," the judge said. "DA Wozniak, have you seen this paperwork yet?"

"I have, Your Honor. It was faxed to my office prior to my coming here."

"Do you have a bail recommendation?"

"Because of the nature of the alleged crimes, I would recommend that we remand the defendant without bail."

"So ordered. We'll set the preliminary hearing for next Tuesday at 10:00 a.m."

With a bang of the judge's gavel, the arraignment was closed. Court security led a dazed and surprised Walt from the courtroom. He would now go to jail to await the outcome of his case.

CHAPTER TWENTY-THREE

Joanie Deerhunter-Powers had just gotten her children to bed. She curled up on the couch with her husband to watch the late news. This was her favorite time of day—when all was quiet, the daily chores were done, and she and Paul could spend some quiet time together catching up on the day's events.

As the newscaster began with the day's top story, Joanie leaned forward, placing both feet on the floor. Her hands tightly gripped the edge of the seat cushion, making her knuckles turn white.

"What's the matter?" Paul asked, suddenly alarmed.

"Turn that up," Joanie said, her voice raised higher than normal. "That's the guy! That's the guy who kidnapped me!" She pointed to the television where a mugshot of Walt filled the screen. Blackness lined the outer edges of her vision, leaving nothing but Walt's face in the center. She began to tremble, as if she was sitting in a snowbank in nothing but her underwear. A cold sweat broke out across her forehead.

"Oh, my god!" Paul wrapped her in a hug to comfort her.

The couple watched in silence as the newscaster explained that the police had arrested Walter Pyke that morning on multiple kidnapping and rape charges, and authorities were currently holding him in the local jail.

Paul and Joanie had been together for the past ten years. The first five years, she kept the abuse to herself, but one night, after a bit too much wine, the entire story came tumbling out. She'd never told anyone before, but since opening up, she'd told him countless times the story of her sexual abuse at the hands of a kidnapper.

Once she finally unburdened herself, she buried herself in Paul's safe embrace. From then on, that's what he was to her more than anything—safe. He had always listened with compassion, willing to give her a hug or let her talk through the pain.

"I was finally at the point in my life where I could get past him. I've worked so hard to put what he did to me behind me." Joanie covered her face with her hands and quietly sobbed. Paul tightened his arms around her shoulders.

"How many women did he do that to?" she wondered out loud. "How many women did he kidnap and hold in that dungeon so he could rape them every stinking day? There must have been others if he's got so many charges, right? Oh, my God.

Maybe if I had gone to the police twelve years ago, this wouldn't have happened."

"You can't say that, sweetheart. It's not your fault. You've always thought there were other women before you he may have abused. They could have said something, and maybe they did. We don't know. But if he threatened the others and their families the way he threatened you, I don't blame them for not speaking up. It looks like this guy got away with it all these years." Paul was clearly trying to find the words that would bring comfort to his wife.

"Do you think it's too late? Should I go to the police now and tell them what he did to me?" Joanie was rocking back and forth, her arms wrapped around her middle.

"If you're up to it, yes, I think you should tell the cops what happened. There's strength in numbers, right? Maybe there *are* other women, and the more women that come forward, the more charges there will be, and he'll get locked up for good. He deserves to spend the rest of his life in jail."

"Okay. Will you go with me?" The tears continued to stream down Joanie's cheeks.

"Of course I will." Paul gently pushed her hair behind her ear and gave her a tender kiss on her temple.

"Can we go tomorrow morning?"

"If you're up to it, sure. We can go right after the kids leave for school and get it over with. How does that sound?"

"Okay." Joanie pulled her legs under her and nestled her head on Paul's chest.

Although the TV was still on, neither one was listening. The thoughts of Walt and the horrific things that took place in the dungeon were filling their heads.

CHAPTER TWENTY-FOUR

For many years, Joanie had tried to force any memories of the bunker, Walt, and the rapes out of her mind, but after seeing his face clearly displayed in her house, on her living room television, the emotions came flooding back.

Her saving grace had always been her husband, Paul. He had never judged her, had never made her feel dirty, and had listened endlessly as she cathartically opened up about her horrifying ordeal. He taught her what love was and gave it to her unconditionally.

When she and Paul first met, her parents were not in favor of their daughter dating Paul. They would have preferred she be with another Native American. But once they got to know Paul and his calm and loving nature, they couldn't be happier for Joanie.

The young couple's dreams were fulfilled when their children were born. Savannah was now eight years old, and Tristan was five. Joanie loved being a wife and mother, and she decided she didn't have time to wallow in the past, so she put all her energy into her family.

Their love had helped her heal. As time went on, she pushed Walt, the sexual abuse, and the dungeon further and further from her thoughts, until she only occasionally thought of her ordeal.

After watching the news about Walt's arrest, Joanie slept fitfully during the night. Seeing Walt's face displayed on the TV, invading the safety and security of her own home, was almost too much to bear. But Paul, clearly sensing her fears, held her throughout the night.

They both slept only a little, so with the new day dawning, they reluctantly got out of bed. They were exhausted but went through the motions of showering and dressing. Neither one was hungry for breakfast, choosing instead to get their energy from several cups of coffee.

Finally, with the kids washed, fed, and loaded onto the school bus, it was time to leave for the police department.

"Will you stay with me?" Joanie asked, as they got in their truck.

"Of course I will. I'll stay with you the whole time, okay?" He reached over and grabbed her hand, curling his fingers around hers and squeezing.

"Let's do this. I can't let that bastard win." Joanie held her head high as she looked at her husband.

"That's my girl." Paul gave her a big smile, giving her the strength she knew she would need to tell her story.

At the police department, Joanie approached the civilian clerk sitting at the front desk. The name plate identified her as Anita.

"Hi, can I help you?" Anita asked.

"Yes, I'd like to talk to an officer, please."

"Can I ask what this is regarding?" Anita said with a kind smile.

Joanie had to bite her bottom lip to stop it from quivering. "I saw on TV last night that you arrested a guy named Walter Pyke for kidnapping and raping several women. I've never talked to the police about it before, but I want to report that he did the same thing to me about fifteen years ago."

The woman behind the counter hesitated for just a moment to process what Joanie was telling her. She stood up to open the door to the office. "Come with me, please."

Anita ushered Joanie and Paul into a conference room and motioned to the chairs surrounding the table. "If you would like to sit here for just a moment, I'll see if I can find Sgt. Steve MacIntosh for you. He's heading the investigation, so I think you should talk to him."

Mac was surprised when Anita burst into the CID office. He, Coop, and Heidi were at their desks. "I've got a woman that just came in, saying Pyke held her captive about fifteen years ago. I thought you'd want to talk to her, so I've already brought her into the conference room."

"Excellent! She may be our missing link. Thank you, Anita. Heidi," Mac looked her way, "I'd like you to come in with me and talk to her.

"I'm with you, Sarge," Heidi said as she grabbed a notebook and pen.

"Coop, do you mind sitting this one out? If she never reported this, she's probably scared and uncomfortable talking about it. I don't want to overwhelm her with too many people."

"I don't mind. I've got a lot of paperwork to do, anyway," answered Coop. He picked up his slice of breakfast pizza and held it high as a salute.

Mac and Heidi took a seat at the conference room table opposite Joanie and Paul. Mac introduced Heidi and himself to Joanie and Paul. Paul made the introductions on behalf of himself and Joanie. She sat quietly, her hands in her lap, while Paul wrapped his arm protectively around her shoulder.

"Thank you for coming in, Joanie." Mac began. "This might be a painful topic to discuss, but I want to assure you that your testimony will help put Walt behind bars, hopefully for the rest of his life."

Almost imperceptibly, Joanie nodded her head.

"Why don't you start by telling us what happened from the beginning. How did he find you and kidnap you?"

"It was just before Halloween, fifteen years ago. I had gone to the store to get some things to make my little brother's Halloween costume. I had been upset about something stupid. I don't even remember what it was. Then this guy—Walt—pulled up and said he noticed I'd been upset, so he offered to drive me home. Only he didn't take me home. He took me to his house."

"Did you get in the car willingly?"

Joanie seemed to have a hard time forming the words. "Yes, I did. He looked like a nice guy, an older guy, and I thought because he was older, I could trust him. Old people are supposed to be nice. At least, I thought so." She looked at her hands in her lap.

"When you realized he wasn't taking you home, did you ask him to turn around or stop the car?" Mac asked.

"Yes, quite a bit. I kept asking him to go back, but he wouldn't. He just kept driving in the wrong direction."

"Can you tell us what happened when he got you to his house?"

Joanie closed her eyes and took a deep breath. Paul rubbed her back slowly and rhythmically, a calming motion that appeared to help. After a moment, she resumed her story. "He led me through the house and into the basement. He had shelves filled with a ton of bottles and cans down there, and at the other end of the basement, he pulled a shelving unit away from the wall. It was really weird because it was the only shelf that didn't have anything on it. There was another door and then a tunnel behind that. He made me climb into the tunnel and it came out in this underground room, which he told me is really an old bomb shelter. He always called it a bunker, but I thought of it as a dungeon. Anyway, I had to go down a small stepladder to get into it." The tears flowed down Joanie's cheeks in a steady stream. Her husband kept rubbing her back, the concern evident in his eyes.

"What happened next?" asked Mac.

"He showed me around the dungeon. There was a tub, a toilet seat on a metal frame—like old people use when they have to go to the bathroom—that had a bucket underneath it. And in a different room... was a mattress." Joanie began crying harder and had a hard time talking. "He pushed me down on the mattress. He handcuffed me to the wall. Then he raped me."

Mac waited a few moments. "Joanie, would you like to take a break?"

"No. No, I need to get this done. I'm okay. Let's keep going."

"Can you tell us if there was any graffiti on the walls?" Heidi asked.

"I don't think so." Joanie frowned as she tried to remember. "No, there wasn't any graffiti on the walls."

Mac nodded his head. That would coincide with Gabrielle's statement that she'd been the one to paint the various expressions on the walls. Gabrielle had been held in the bunker after Joanie.

"Can you tell me about a typical day in the bunker?" Heidi asked.

"He wanted sex at least once every day, usually late morning when he brought lunch. Then, on some days, he would have me take a bath. Some days I brushed my teeth. He gave me a calendar to mark a B for bath and T for teeth. I also had to mark an S for sex. Every day had an S.

"He told me I had to have sex with him or else he would go after my family. I remember one day after I'd been there for a few months, he showed me a couple pictures that really scared me. One was a picture from the inside of my house, with my mom standing at the stove. He also had a picture of my little brother sitting on the couch and another one of my father washing the car."

"How did he get inside the house to take those pictures?" Mac was curious about that bit of information.

"He said he told my mother that the landlord had asked him to check for leaky pipes. That terrified me because I'd given him my address when I thought he was driving me home, so he obviously knew where I lived. That's why I believed his threats and didn't report him to the police after I was released."

"Did he tell you about a sex club he belonged to?" Mac asked.

"Yes. He said he and a bunch of powerful men belonged to a sex club. He said he was friends with the chief of police, a bunch of politicians, and even celebrities. He said they all belonged to this sex club and his job was to train me to have good sex. When he thought I was ready, he would turn me over to these men, and then I was supposed to have sex with them.

I was so scared he would do that. He even showed me a police officer's badge that the chief gave him."

"How did you escape?" Heidi asked.

"I'd been held for almost three years when he came in one morning and said he wanted me to go with him to California because he had some personal business to take care of. I guess he bought some land out there and needed to go sign some papers. Anyway, he said no one knew about me living in the dungeon, so there wasn't anyone he could ask to bring me food, and he couldn't leave me alone for those couple days, so we both went to California.

"The strange thing was that his son, Gregory, drove us to the airport. He'd been waiting in the house, and when I showed up in the living room with Walt, Gregory looked really surprised. Walt told him some bullshit about me having an eating disorder and he was trying to coach me into getting better. I don't think Gregory believed him because he kept giving Walt the stink eye.

"Then, after Gregory went out to the car, Walt stayed behind with me for a minute. He blindfolded me while we were still in the house so I couldn't see anything on the way to the car. He said he didn't want me to see where he lived or the other girls that lived there."

"There were other girls?" Heidi asked, surprised.

"Not that I ever saw or heard. If there were other girls, they must have been in the main part of the house. Walt was the only person who ever went into the dungeon while I was there."

"What happened in California?" Mac asked.

"It was the first time I'd ever been on a plane. I hate to say it, but it was pretty cool. It was the first time I'd ever flown in an airplane, and I enjoyed it. I'm just sorry it had to be with him. Anyway, we were only there for a day. We stayed in a hotel overnight, and then we had to go to a lawyer's office the next morning to sign the papers. He told me to sit there with my mouth shut and not say a word. We flew back home after that appointment.

"Then, after we got back, we were walking in the airport and he just stopped. He gave me a couple of quarters and told me to call someone for a ride. I was free. He was letting me go. I couldn't believe it. It was as simple as that. Before he could change his mind, I ran like hell, found a pay phone and called my parents. They picked me up at the airport, and I went home."

"I have to ask, Joanie, why didn't you report this sooner?" Mac asked as gently as he could.

"I know. I should have, and I'm so very sorry about that, but I was scared. He said he would hurt my family if I went to the police." Joanie looked down at her hands in her lap.

"No one is blaming you, so please don't feel like you did anything wrong. This guy got away with it for a lot of years because of threats like that. He knows how to manipulate his victims. That's what predators like him do." Mac looked at her with compassion in his eyes. "You're doing the right thing by coming to us now."

"Is there anything else you can think of?" Heidi asked softly.

"Yeah, there is one thing. It was kind of strange, but he wanted to read the Bible with me every day. I don't know why, unless he wanted to convert me. He kept asking about my religion as a Native American, and he said it wasn't a real religion. He said *his* religion and the god *he* worshiped was the one true god."

Joanie looked between Mac and Heidi. "Paul is the only one I've ever told my story to. Not even my parents know the truth, but I have to admit, even though I've kept this secret for years, and I've struggled emotionally for that entire time, I feel better now. It feels like the weight of the world has been lifted off my shoulders. I'm glad he finally got caught."

Mac gave her a reassuring smile and stood up from the table. "If you don't mind waiting a few minutes, Joanie, I'll type up your statement and have you sign it."

"That's fine, Sergeant. We'll wait right here," Joanie said as she looked at her husband. Paul gave her hand a gentle squeeze.

When Mac and Heidi returned to the CID office, Mac got right to work at his desk, typing Joanie's statement. After carefully typing the statement and double-checking it for accuracy, he returned to the conference room to have Joanie review her typed version. She signed the form, giving her approval of what was written, and Mac walked her to the front door.

"I know it wasn't easy after all this time, but I appreciate you coming forward." Mac held out his hand and gave Joanie and Paul firm handshakes.

"Sergeant, how many women have come forward? How many others did he kidnap?" Joanie asked.

"You're the fifth victim that we know of," Mac said. Joanie slowly nodded her head. Paul put his arm over Joanie's shoulder as they left the police department.

Mac returned to the CID office, subdued by the interview with Joanie. While he had been busy typing Joanie's statement and seeing her out, Heidi filled Coop in on the interview with Joanie Deerhunter-Powers.

Heidi looked over at Mac when he slumped into his chair. "Mac, I can't imagine what these women went through," she said.

"Here's a question," Coop said. "We now know that Joanie was taken in 2008 and then released in 2011, but the next victim wasn't kidnapped until 2015. What happened between 2011 and 2015?"

"That's a good question," Mac said. "Now that he has been arraigned and has an attorney, we can't talk to him anymore, but I can ask District Attorney Wozniak to have a conversation with Pyke while his attorney is present. We need to know if there were more victims during that time that haven't come forward, or, God forbid, if someone died. Maybe he just had a dry spell for some reason, but I tend to doubt that. Now, if you'll excuse me, I'm going to draw up the paperwork the judge will need to arraign Walt on the additional charges for Joanie. That will bring him to a total of five counts each of the same charges that he has from the other women's cases." Mac greedily rubbed his hands together.

"I hope he gets life in front of the firing squad," Coop said. Mac and Heidi both looked at Coop, trying to figure out if he meant what he had said. His expression was unreadable. With a shrug of her shoulders and a smirk raising the corners of her mouth, Heidi returned to her desk.

CHAPTER TWENTY-FIVE

Sergeant MacIntosh typed up the paperwork the judge would need when she arraigned Walt on the additional charges of kidnapping, rape, and sexual misconduct involving Joanie Deerhunter-Powers. He and Coop would take it all down to the Courthouse for Judge Johannsen.

After a short drive to the courthouse with Coop behind the wheel of the department-issued vehicle, Mac and Coop arrived at Judge Johannsen's office. The judge was at lunch, but her clerk was still at her desk. They handed over the paperwork on behalf of Walter Pyke's fifth kidnapping victim. She assured the detectives the judge would receive the paperwork as soon as she came back from her lunch break.

"C'mon, let's grab some lunch," Coop said as they left the courthouse. "What are you in the mood for?"

Mac, who had walked briskly to claim the driver's seat before Coop could, pulled the car from the parking lot onto the main street. "How about Sandy's Diner? It's right here."

"I was hoping you'd say that," said Coop. "I could go for one of her juicy cheeseburgers with a huge side of loaded fries and a nice, cold iced tea."

Mac found a rare parking spot right in front of the diner as another car pulled away from the curb.

"I think I'll stick to a grilled cheese sandwich and a bowl of tomato soup," said Mac.

They were able to find an open table right next to the front window, and before long, Ginger, the long-time waitress, brought glasses of water to the table. "Hi, Sergeant Macintosh, Investigator Cooper. How are you?"

"Doing well, Ginger. How are you?" Mac said.

"Great! How about you, Ginger?" echoed Coop.

"Oh, you know how it is... I'm a day older but still standing and still smiling," said Ginger, chuckling. "Are you ready to order, or do you need another minute?"

The investigators gave their orders. While they waited for the food to arrive, their conversation naturally turned to the Walter Pyke case.

"I can't help but wonder if there were women he held hostage during the gaps, especially between Joanie and Gabrielle. That's about four years when we can't account for any victims. At least, not yet." Coop had picked up the wrapper from his straw and was absent-mindedly tearing it into little pieces.

"The way I see it, one of three things happened," said Mac as he held up a finger to tick off each idea.

"Number one, something happened in his personal life that prevented him from holding anyone in the bunker; number two, he had at least one hostage during that time, but she hasn't come forward, or number three, he had at least one hostage, but she died."

"Let's hope it's not curtain number three," said Coop.

"Maybe Walt's son knew...." Mac let his comment hang in the air. "From what the first victim, Joanie Deerhunter-Powers, said, the son drove her and Walter to the airport. It would make sense that he knew something was up with his old man."

Coop stroked his chin, deep in thought. "If that's the case, we'll need to have a little chat with him, to find out. We can always charge him as an accessory if it turns out he knew about the girls and what his father was doing to them in the bunker."

"Let's see if we can't find him after lunch," Mac said.

"Agreed," Coop said.

Their lunch arrived as their conversation turned to the upcoming major league baseball games. Mac and Coop dove into their food with gusto, while enjoying a few minutes of their favorite topic of conversation—sports.

Just as they were finishing their meal, Mac's phone rang. The caller ID showed it was District Attorney Dennis Wozniak on the line.

"Hi, Dennis. How are you?"

"I'm doing well. Thank you for asking."

"Coop is here with me. Can I put you on speaker?"

"Absolutely. You should both hear this."

Mac turned on the speaker but lowered the volume so only he and Coop could hear Dennis and not the other customers.

Dennis got right to the point. "I thought you'd like to know. I met with Walter Pyke and his attorney, Declan Murphy, at the jail this morning. We asked him about his victims, and he was still claiming there were only four. We reminded him that, with Joanie Deerhunter-Powers coming forward, that made five victims, so he finally relented and agreed there were five victims. I asked him a number of times if there were any more than that, but he insisted there were only five.

"I asked why there was such a large gap in-between Joanie and Gabrielle, and he said his son, Gregory, had separated from his wife and moved back home. He had been living with Walt during that entire time. Gregory and the wife eventually divorced, and that's when he moved out of Walter's house again. At least, that's what Walter is claiming, but he doesn't exactly have a great track record with honesty.

He may very well be lying again. I would ask that you get a hold of the son and see if his story coincides with his father's.

"We can do that," said Mac.

"Walter claims his son did not know at any point that he'd kept women hostage in the bunker. Walter said he was concerned that if he told his son about the women, Gregory would want to have sex with them, and Walter didn't want to share the women; his words, not mine."

"There was a gap of three or four years between Yen and Emily," Coop said. "Did he say anything about that?"

"No, he refused to say anything about that particular time, no matter how many times or how many ways I asked. But if you can believe this one, he kept saying he thought he would spend, at most, a couple days in jail, maybe pay a small fine or perform a few hours of community service. He doesn't seem to understand the severity of the crimes. He insisted he took care of the women, that they, in his words, 'didn't want for anything.' He thinks that as long as he brought them food once or twice a day and gave them a staticky radio to listen to, it was perfectly fine to kidnap these women, hold them against their will, and force them to have sex with him."

"Unbelievable!" said Coop, slapping the table for emphasis.

"That's ridiculous," said Mac. "How can anyone think that's okay?"

"He's going to be in for a big surprise when he learns that if he's found guilty after a trial, the court could sentence him to life in prison. And considering the witness statements, his own admissions, and the evidence, especially the bunker itself, I have no doubt he'll be found guilty. I intend to prosecute this case to the fullest so that he doesn't spend another day as a free man ever again."

CHAPTER TWENTY-SIX

Mac and Coop had the statements from the five victims, as well as Walter Pyke's statement admitting to taking the women, but it would be even better if they had more evidence. They wanted to make sure they had an iron-clad case that would put him in jail for the rest of his days.

Their first stop was to see Walt's son, Gregory. They were hoping he would be at home since he was on disability and unable to work. According to a background check, he had fallen off a roof years before and suffered a broken back. The roofing company he'd worked for paid dearly after an OSHA investigation proved there was negligence when Gregory had not been wearing a tether when he fell.

As they parked in front of Gregory's address, Mac and Coop looked at the tan, two-story Craftsman house with a spacious front porch that ran the length of the home. The lawn was well-maintained, with professional-looking landscaping and a manicured lawn. Along the outer edges of the home were rows of rose bushes in colorful pinks, reds, and yellows.

"It looks like Gregory shares his father's fondness for roses," Coop said.

"Let's hope that's all they have in common," Mac countered.

As they approached the house, the front door opened before they'd stepped off the sidewalk. A large man in a plaid flannel shirt stood in the doorway. "What do you want? I ain't buying anything, so you might as well leave now."

Mac and Coop both wore their badges on the front of their belts. They simultaneously moved their suit coats to the side, exposing their gold shields.

"Mr. Pyke?" asked Mac.

"Yeah, what do you want?"

"My name is Investigator MacIntosh, this is Investigator Cooper. We just have a couple of questions for you, if you have a minute."

Pyke stood still for several uncomfortable seconds. Mac and Coop watched him carefully. He finally moved to the side and motioned with his hand, inviting the investigators inside. "I suppose this has something to do with my father."

Relieved that he wasn't going to slam the door in their faces, Mac and Coop followed him into the living room.

Pyke invited the detectives to have a seat as he slowly lowered himself into a recliner. Mac and Coop sat on the sofa. They both pulled a small notebook and a pen from the inside pocket of their suit coats.

"So, you're aware we arrested your father for kidnapping and holding women hostage in the underground bunker at his house," Mac began.

"He called me from jail and told me about it."

"Did you know about the bunker?"

"Yeah, I knew about it, but I hadn't gone down there in years. My folks bought the house when I was five or six years old. I remember going down with my father to see it not long after we moved in, but it was damp and smelly, and there were a ton of spiderwebs all over. As a little kid, it freaked me out, so that was about the only time I'd ever been in it. I guess after all these years, I forgot about it."

"Did you know anything about the women he'd held in the bunker?"

"Definitely not. Not at all."

"You lived with him for a while, didn't you? Did he hang out in the bunker at all when you were there?" Coop asked.

"Yes, I lived with him, but it was quite a long time ago. My wife and I had separated. I was working a crappy job and couldn't afford my own place, so I had no choice but to move in with him. My ex ended up taking me for everything I had in the divorce. It took a while, but because I was living with him, I managed to save up some money and bought a dump of a house."

"This house?" Coop asked, wide-eyed as he looked around. "I wouldn't call it a dump."

"No, not this house." Gregory chuckled. "I fell off a roof a few years ago and got a nice settlement. I used a portion of the money to buy this house."

Mac did a quick calculation in his head. The house must have run at least $400,000, so if that was only a portion of the settlement, Pyke must have gotten a bundle.

"I also had to live with him for about a year while I recuperated from the fall. I hated it, but I had no choice. Anyway," Gregory continued, "he would go downstairs to the basement, but he had an enormous collection of bottles and cans. I always figured he was down there doing whatever it was he did with all that stuff. When I found out he was keeping women in the bunker, I was really surprised. I had no idea."

"Have you ever met any of the women that he held hostage?" Mac and Coop already knew from Joanie Deerhunter-Powers that Gregory had driven Walt and Joanie to the airport, but they wanted him to tell them about it.

"Yeah, once I did, but I didn't know she was living in the bunker, and I sure as hell didn't know what he was doing to her. She was just a kid." Gregory shook his head, his eyebrows knit together.

"How did you happen to meet her?"

"My father was going to California to sign some paperwork because he bought some apartment building or some land or something out there. I don't remember the details. But he called me and asked if I would drive him to the airport. When I got to the house to pick him up, he came into the living room with this young girl on his arm."

"What did he say about her? How did he explain her presence?" Coop asked.

"He said something ridiculous, that she had an eating disorder or something, and he was trying to coach her into eating right. I knew it was a bunch of bullshittery because he lives on junk food himself and never eats vegetables or fruits. He's in no position to teach anyone how to eat right.

"Then he goes and puts a blindfold on this girl before she even leaves the house. Once we got in the car, I asked him what in hell was going on, but he stuck to the 'coaching her to eat right' story." Gregory used air quotes with his fingers for emphasis.

"Did he explain why he had to blindfold her?" Coop asked.

"Yeah, he referred to his house as a half-way house, or something like that. He said he had to protect the location, so he supposedly told her they were out in the middle of nowhere, miles away from any kind of civilization. He said he'd told her if she didn't know where she was, she shouldn't try to run away. It all sounded wrong to me, but he stuck to that story.

"How do you and your father get along?" Mac asked.

"Okay, I guess. When I was in high school, I never brought any girlfriends home because he would flirt with them. It was embarrassing. He would comment on their clothes, tell them how pretty they were, and stare at their chests. I lost a couple of girlfriends because of him so I stopped bringing them home. It's hindsight, but now I know he did it because he's a pervert.

"Is there anything else you can tell us about him?" said Coop.

"He always wants things to go his way and believes he's always right, so I make an effort to stay out of his way and avoid situations where I might seem like I'm challenging his authority. I was raised with him telling me to do things because he said so. If I defied him, I got smacked around a bit. Not anything bad. Every once in a while, he would cuff me on the side of my head, but it was light enough that it never hurt me. Mostly, it was just verbal stuff between the two of us. Me getting mouthy and my father trying to show his authority and that he knows everything.

"You have an older brother, right?"

"Yes, he's six years older than I am. He moved to Chicago for college, and other than summer breaks, he never came back. He couldn't stand my father, so once he graduated from college, he stayed out there. I talk to him once in a while, but I haven't laid eyes on him in years. As far as I know, he hasn't talked to my father at all in years."

"How about your mother and father's relationship?" Mac asked. "Did they get along?"

"My mother was a saint." Gregory smiled at the thought. "She always kept the peace and never argued with him. She made him believe that whatever he said, goes. But sometimes she agreed to do whatever he wanted, and then, when he wasn't paying attention, she would do whatever *she* wanted to do, especially where I was concerned. Like, if I had done something wrong, and he said I had to go to bed without dinner. Later on, she would sneak upstairs with a sandwich, a big piece of cake, and an ice-cold glass of milk.

"She had dinner on the table at six o'clock sharp and everything was homemade. She never served takeout food or canned food, nothing like that. Even the vegetables came from a garden out back, and she froze or canned everything she grew. The house was always spotless, too. She was always cleaning the floors and dusting the furniture.

"But when I started getting older and would get mouthy with my father, she would step in. She wouldn't talk back to him, but she would say it was time I took my bath, or it was time for bed, or I had homework I had to do. Then she would make me go upstairs to my room and tell me if I stayed out of his way for a bit, then everything would be okay."

"Was he ever physically abusive to her?" Mac asked.

"As far as I know, he never laid a hand on her. I think if he had, she would have left him. That's something she wouldn't have put up with. She hated it when he smacked me, but she knew it wasn't hard enough to hurt, so she just kept quiet about it. I think if she had spoken up, he would have had a screaming fit with her, so it was best to keep the peace by just letting it go. Then she got sick and, unfortunately, passed away in 2007."

"It doesn't look like your mother would have known about the women in the bunker. He kidnapped his first victim in 2008," said Mac.

"I think if she knew about that, she would have turned him in to the police or something. She never would have allowed him to hurt those women like that. Never.

"After he got arrested, I remembered something I hadn't thought about in years. He had remodeled the bathroom shortly before my mother got sick. There was an old claw-foot tub he wanted to get rid of and he asked me to help him drag it into the bunker. It was heavy as hell, and we struggled with it, but eventually we got it down there. I asked him why he wanted to drag it into the bunker and not take it to the dump, but he never answered me. He just told me to shut the hell up and help him.

"When the bunker was built, there was a hallway in the basement that led right to it, but I was down there a few years ago and noticed that the entrance wasn't there anymore. I asked him what happened to the bunker, and he said he had it all filled in with dirt, including the hallway. He can be eccentric, so I just chalked it up to that. I gave up trying to figure him out years ago.

"I found out after he was arrested that it obviously hadn't been filled in, but for some reason, he had piled concrete bricks in that hallway to make it smaller, more like a tunnel you have to crawl through, and he installed doors and a metal shelf to block the entrance. I guess now I know what he was doing."

After a few more questions, Mac and Coop thanked Gregory and left his home.

"Do you think Gregory is telling the truth, that he didn't know about the women in the bunker?" Coop asked.

"I could be wrong, but judging by his answers, I don't think he did. He looked us square in the eyes when he answered our questions and never flinched. He didn't stutter or stammer, and his body language told me he was telling the truth. What do you think?"

Coop agreed that Gregory seemed to have no idea about the kidnapped women or that his father was such a monster. Although there didn't appear to be any love lost between the father and son, it must have come as a huge shock for Gregory to hear about the women his father held against their will for his own sexual pleasure.

CHAPTER TWENTY-SEVEN

For several days after Walter's arrest, the evidence technicians scoured Walter Pyke's home on Battle Creek Road for every bit of evidence they could find. They took photos of the entire house but concentrated on the bunker, its contents, and the graffiti on the walls. Things they could carry, like the mattress, radio, and potty, were brought back to the police department. Some articles would be held simply as evidence, other items would be tested for DNA evidence. They also dusted everything within reach for fingerprints. It took the technicians over eighteen hours total to gather the evidence.

Mac and Coop went back to the neighborhood to talk to Walt's neighbors. They knocked on the door of the house to the right of his home. A middle-aged woman with a flowered house dress came to the door with what appeared to be a glass of wine in her hand. It was eleven o'clock in the morning.

"Hi, ma'am. I'm Investigator Cooper and this is Sergeant MacIntosh. We're with the Gaithersburg Police Department, and we'd like to ask you a few questions about one of your neighbors, if you have a moment."

"Sure, what can I help you with?" she answered politely. She didn't hide the fact that she was eyeballing Coop from head to toe. She leaned seductively against the doorjamb, her flirtatious smile showing that she liked what she saw.

Coop's cheeks burned bright red, a sign that he had picked up on her appraisal of him. "Do you know your neighbor, Walter Pyke?" he asked, as he took a small notebook from his suit coat pocket.

"Yes, I've lived next door to him for about five years now. What's he done?"

"What can you tell us about him?" continued Mac.

"Well, he's pretty strange, I'd say. He has beautiful rose gardens and the first year or so that I was here, if I saw him working in the yard while I was out for a walk, I would wave to him, you know, to be friendly, but he always ignored me. He'd look me square in the eye and act like I wasn't even there. They never put up Christmas lights and they turned the porch light off at Halloween. Can you believe that?"

"Did you ever see people coming and going from his house?" Coop asked.

"Not really. I don't recall ever seeing anyone visit him. It's like he had no friends at all. He's got a son that's just as weird as he is, though. He doesn't live there and doesn't even visit his father very often. Maybe once every month or so, is all. I only see Walt once in a while because I can't really see into their yard. The bushes are too high." The woman craned her neck to look at Walt's yard, as if to show that she couldn't see through the bushes.

"Why do you say the son is also weird?" Mac asked.

"He doesn't seem very friendly either. I try to be a nice neighbor, say hello and ask how their day is going, but neither one of them wants any part of it. The son might give me a quick wave hello, but that's about it. They're really anti-social."

Coop asked her name and wrote it down in his notebook.

"Don't you want my phone number?" she asked Coop, with wide eyes and a hopeful smile.

"Uh, no, that's okay, ma'am. That's not necessary for our report. Thank you, ma'am. Have a nice day." Coop's blush returned to his cheeks.

The investigators turned to walk down the porch steps when the woman called out to them. "Hey, you never said what he did."

Neither of them answered her.

Coop and Mac then went to the house on the other side of the woman they had just spoken to and doubled back to check on the residence to the left of Walter's home, but no one answered either door. They visited a few more homes on the street and about half of the residents answered the knocks on their doors. The rest didn't appear to be home.

Of those neighbors they spoke with, the general consensus was that Walt kept to himself and didn't like to communicate with the neighbors. He wasn't disliked, by any means; most people just shrugged their shoulders and admitted they knew little about the man.

Most of the residents admitted they had seen the news and were aware of the situation. They tried questioning the investigators, fishing for more details of the horrendous story, but Mac and Coop refused to answer their inquiries and spun the questions back to the neighbors without releasing any of the details the neighbors were searching for. As the investigation continued, they would get their answers soon enough when the media released the updates.

CHAPTER TWENTY-EIGHT

No matter how hard Defense Attorney Declan Murphy tried, he could not make Walt fully understand why it was wrong to kidnap women, hold them hostage in an underground bunker where they were cut off from friends and family, and force them to have sex with him on a continual, daily basis. According to Walt, as long as the women were provided with food, water, a bath, and a make-shift toilet, it was okay. He believed that as long as he provided the basic necessities of life, he wasn't doing anything morally or lawfully wrong.

At Declan Murphy's request, Judge Johannsen ordered a psychiatrist to examine Walt and ensure his mental competence to stand trial. The psychiatrist met with Walt and, after speaking to him at length, determined that, although Walt did not agree with the charges, he understood them. The psychiatrist determined he was competent to stand trial.

Eventually, Murphy was able to convince Walt that, given the public outrage and the insurmountable evidence, he would be much better off taking a plea deal than going to trial. The District Attorney had already promised the sentence would be the same either way, but with a plea deal, at least it wouldn't be a long, dragged-out affair. DA Wozniak had emphasized that he would prefer to spare the victims from testifying, but if they had to go to trial, he would ask them to take the stand.

After several meetings with his attorney, Walter Pyke finally consented to a plea deal. There would be no trial. Two months after his arrest, the jail deputies brought him to court to stand in front of Judge Johannsen and plead to five counts of first-degree kidnapping. The remaining charges would be dismissed.

He was wearing the tan jail shirt, pants, and canvas slip-on shoes that signified he was a prisoner. They bound his wrists together with handcuffs and attached them to a chain that encircled his waist.

Curious onlookers, as well as reporters from the various news outlets, filled the courtroom gallery. Walt's story had become headline news, even at the national level.

Walt's family members were missing from the courtroom. His sons had had no contact with him since his arrest and obviously wanted nothing to do with him. Walt had received no visitors while he was in jail other than his attorney.

As Walt and Declan Murphy stood in front of the judge, she asked if he would be entering a plea to the charges. "Yes, Your Honor, I plead guilty."

Judge Johannsen asked, before she would accept Walt's plea of guilty, if he understood the charges.

"Yes, Your Honor," Walt said. "I understand the charges. I just don't agree with them. I gave the ladies everything they wanted. I took good care of them. The only thing I asked for in return was that they have sex with me. That's a basic right of every man to have sex whenever he wants, right?"

Murphy, who was standing beside Walt, jabbed his elbow into Walt's side. "We went through this," he whispered to his client. "You need to answer the judge. She will not accept your plea until you acknowledge that you understand the charges and weren't coerced into pleading guilty."

Judge Johannsen waited for Murphy to finish conversing with Walt. "Mr. Pyke, I believe your attorney has gone over this with you a number of times. My question to you requires either a yes or no answer. I will ask you again. Do you understand the charges?"

"Yes, Judge." Walt said with a sigh. "I understand the charges."

"And are you voluntarily and knowingly entering a plea of guilty of your own free will?"

"Yes, Your Honor."

"I will order a pre-sentence report, and we'll see you in six weeks for sentencing." With a bang of her gavel, the plea proceedings were complete, and Walt was led by the officers back to jail.

Six weeks later, Walt was brought to the court to be sentenced for his crimes by Judge Johannsen. Members of local and national news media were crowding the gallery, eager to report on the sentencing. It was standing room only.

Walt sat nervously in the holding cell next to the courtroom. When his name was called, the bailiff notified court security that he could be brought before the judge.

As Walt entered the courtroom, he glanced at the people filling the seats of the gallery. He was surprised to see that every seat had been occupied. In the back, news people had set up cameras on tripods to film the proceedings. He also recognized a familiar face—known to him as Joanie Deerhunter, in the front row, glaring at him. He smiled at her, but she did not return the smile. Instead, Joanie greeted him with a look of hatred.

The jail deputy escorted Walt to the defense table, where his attorney was already waiting. Judge Johannsen asked Murphy if he was ready to proceed. The attorney stood and said they were.

Dennis Wozniak acknowledged the same; the prosecution was ready to proceed.

Judge Johannsen asked DA Wozniak if he'd like to make a sentencing recommendation. Dennis stood at the podium centered in front of the judge, cleared his throat, and began speaking.

"Your Honor, Mr. Pyke has been kidnapping women and holding them hostage in his underground bomb shelter for at least the last fifteen years, strictly for his own selfish and sexual pleasure. He is a serial kidnapper and rapist. These women were each held for anywhere from a few months to over three years. While he held them, they were forced to sever ties with their families and friends. They lost their dignity and sometimes their innocence. He's left these women fragile, broken, and damaged in ways that we can't even imagine. Judge, the people would like to ask for a maximum sentence of eighteen years to life."

"Thank you, DA Wozniak," the judge said. "Counselor, would you like to address the court?" The judge was looking at Attorney Murphy.

"Yes, Your Honor. Thank you." Murphy took a deep breath before he began. "Mr. Pyke firmly believed he was being kind to the women in his care. He gave them food, water, access to bathroom facilities, and entertainment in the form of magazines and a radio. He even brought a couple of the women with him when he ran errands.

"Mr. Pyke tried hard to make the women feel appreciated. He called them his 'Little Flowers' or 'Little Roses,' which were terms of endearment to him. The idea that he was doing something wrong never occurred to him.

"Based on his lack of intent, I would ask that the Court consider a lesser sentence. Thank you, Your Honor," Murphy said as he returned to his seat at the defense table, his shoulders slumped. He knew his request for a lighter sentence would only be a waste of time and that the court would not honor it. But whether he liked it or not, his obligation as defense counsel was to plead for mercy on behalf of his client.

The judge then asked Joanie Deerhunter-Powers if she would like to speak. Joanie gave a quick nod of acknowledgement, and with a sheet of paper tightly clenched in her hand, she approached the podium. Her husband Paul went up with her. He stood next to her and gently rubbed her back. Joanie took a moment, her eyes tightly closed, to compose herself. With a deep cleansing breath, she looked up, ready to pour her heart out to the court.

"Walter Pyke is the devil. He took me when I was walking home from a trip to the store with a promise to give me a ride home. Like a fool, I accepted the ride. I kept telling him to turn around. I asked him to stop the car, but he wouldn't listen. From that point on, my life and my family's lives changed forever.

"He took me to his house, where he had an underground bomb shelter that was built to protect people, but it didn't protect me from Walter Pyke. He locked me in that bunker for more than three years. He fed me only once, maybe twice a day. I took a bath in a few inches of cold water from a garden hose, but only when he allowed me to. I had to use a paint bucket when I had to go to the bathroom. But worst of all, he raped me every single, stinking day. I was only fourteen years old when he kidnapped me. I was a virgin, and no boy had ever kissed me, let alone had sex with me.

"I will never get over what he's done to me, and I'll never be the same person I was before he kidnapped me. He took my innocence. He took my virginity. That was something that should have happened with someone I loved, not Walter Pyke, and I hate Walter Pyke. He didn't have the right to do that to me.

"He robbed me of all that time I could have had with my parents and my little brother. My little brother, Stevie, depended on me. He looked up to me. The day Walter Pyke kidnapped me, I had been shopping for things I needed to make Stevie's Halloween costume. And because Walter Pyke took me that day, Stevie never went trick-or-treating." Joanie hesitated, trying to stop herself from crying. "He hasn't been trick-or-treating since, either. It brings back too many sad feelings for him.

"And the worst part is, I was not the only one. As I understand it, there were at least five of us kidnapped and raped by this monster. If he gets out, he'll keep doing it. Judge, I beg of you, please put Walter Pyke away for good. Please put him in jail and throw away the key. Thank you."

Paul gave Joanie's hand a comforting, supportive squeeze as they left the podium. In return, Joanie gave her husband a nod and a smile that showed she was glad she had confronted her kidnapper. As Joanie walked back to her chair in the front row of the gallery, she appeared to stand a bit taller, holding her head a bit higher, as if she had finally lifted the weight of the world from her shoulders.

"Will the defendant please stand for sentencing," ordered Judge Johannsen. "Mr. Pyke, I have to say, this is one of the most unusual cases I've ever dealt with. It's not very often we hear of someone in this community that has such a disregard for human life. You took not one, not two, but at least five women away from their families and their lives to satisfy your own sexual appetite. You've hurt these women in ways I can't even begin to imagine. You have taken things from them, things you had no right to take— their dignity, their pride, their sexuality, and their freedom. And because of that, I am sentencing you to the maximum allowed by law. You are hereby sentenced to a term of eighteen years to life, and I can honestly say I hope to never find out that you are walking our fine streets ever again.

"I also order you to surrender your assets as restitution. According to the pre-sentence report, you have assets worth approximately $1 million. I am ordering you to surrender your cash, and any property, including your house, will be sold, with the proceeds being divided among the victims. Mr. Pyke, get out of my courtroom."

With a firm bang of the judge's gavel, the court case was closed. The custody deputy wrapped his hand around Walter's elbow to escort him out of the courtroom. Walter snatched his arm away from the deputy. "But, Judge, I don't understand," Walter yelled. "I took good care of them! I even let them have a bubble bath once in a while."

Judge Johannsen never uttered a word as she watched the defendant being led by two large deputies from the courtroom. Walt tried turning back towards the judge, but he couldn't loosen the even tighter grip the deputies now had on his arms.

The room filled with flashes of bright lights and sharp clicks as the members of the media snapped endless pictures of Walter during his tirade as he was led from the courtroom.

Walter Pyke would make the evening news across the country.

EPILOGUE

Walter Pyke had lived a modest life. Before retiring, he did odd jobs and worked as a handyman. He lived frugally in the same out-of-date home for decades, and at the time of his arrest, his net worth was a cool $1 million. As part of his plea deal, authorities confiscated his bank accounts and sold his home and the properties in California, including the property he had purchased when he traveled to California with Joanie Deerhunter-Powers. They then divided the money among the five victims as a form of compensation. Still, it would never make up for what his victims had suffered at his hand.

They sold the bottle and can collection that had been scattered throughout the basement on eBay. This incredible acquisition of 13,000 cans and bottles brought in $500 for the victims.

The home where Walt lived and held women captive for years was sold. Deshawna Washington's brother was the buyer. He bought the home to keep it out of the hands of those who might exploit its history.

Washington also wanted to help the victims heal, and he did that by making arrangements to knock down the bunker. Although the house itself would be left standing, the underground bunker would be destroyed; the concrete walls would be dug up and the space would be filled in with dirt.

On the day the construction equipment arrived to demolish the bunker, Deshawna, Joanie, and Gabrielle stood by and watched. It was the first and only time these ladies would meet. They held each other, their arms tightly intertwined in a group hug. An occasional tear would flow, but the moment proved to be highly cathartic. They would finally get closure and could begin to heal with this chapter of their lives at an end.

Sergeant Steve MacIntosh, Investigator James Cooper, and Investigator Heidi Thompson also stood by to watch the destruction. Regrettably, this case had taken years before the suspect was identified and arrested, and for Sgt. MacIntosh, it was a case that would always stay with him. A part of him felt guilty for not being able to solve it sooner. If he had found Walt after the first victim came forward, he thought, there might have been fewer victims. He would always wonder if there was something he had overlooked, something he could have done differently. But, as they say, "Hindsight is 20/20."

The small crowd stood by, silently watching as the excavator tore into the ground. The first swipe of the bucket easily tore away the grass. The next swipe dug into the soil, exposing the roof of the bunker.

The large machine moved closer to the center of the yard on squeaking treads, the bucket poised over the bed of roses that stood like a solitary island in the middle of the ocean. Another swipe and the beautiful roses were tossed aside to join the growing pile of dirt.

Suddenly, the foreman standing near the excavator frantically ran his finger across his neck, signifying to the heavy equipment operator to stop. Mac, who'd been leaning against his car, straightened when he saw the man's signal.

Mac's eyes focused on the foreman, who was leaning over the newly dug hole, looking into its depth. The foreman waved to Mac as a sign that he wanted Mac to approach. Mac poked an elbow into Coop's side, saying, "Come with me. Heidi, you too."

When they reached the foreman, he simply pointed into the hole and took a step back. Mac, Coop and Heidi looked down into the hollow pit. There, amid the dirt and broken rose stems, was a skull. A human skull.

Heidi covered her mouth with her hand, clearly shocked at the sight. Coop just shook his head.

"Oh, shit," said Mac. "Let's get everyone out of here and call in the medical examiner. This could very well be another victim."

"If it is another victim," said Coop, "it could explain why there were gaps in-between them."

Mac ran his fingers through his hair. "Just when I thought we were done with this asshole," said Mac quietly.

A complete skeleton was found under the rose garden that day. The medical examiner was able to conclude that the bones belonged to a female, although the DNA that was extracted from the bone marrow would not lead to her identity.

Walter Pyke would spend the rest of his life behind bars. He would be denied parole twice before passing away, after having spent more than twenty years in prison.

One has to wonder how he felt about being imprisoned, where he was told when and what to eat, when to shower, and was forced to use a toilet in his cell, when he was in such denial regarding his own victims.

ABOUT THE AUTHOR

LeeAnne James is a multiple award-winning novelist. She grew up in Central New York and spent the last twenty-two years working for the local police department as their administrative clerk. Recently retired, she now makes Southern Pennsylvania her home with her husband and son where she continues to write. *Five Roses for Walter* is her fifth novel. When she's not writing or reading, LeeAnne likes to try out new recipes, especially for dessert.

Note from LeeAnne James

Word-of-mouth is crucial for any author to succeed. If you enjoyed *Five Roses for Walter*, please leave a review online—anywhere you are able. Even if it's just a sentence or two. It would make all the difference and would be very much appreciated.

Thanks!
LeeAnne James